A Warning to the Reader

Some people create their own nightmares. Other people are born into them . . .

This is the strange and chilling story of a nightmare spawned in a flash of lightning. Of creatures brought into this world, cursed from the day they were born. It is the third and final tale of Frankenstein's children. And anyone who has ever felt doomed by forces out of their control will u that plagues the heirs

It is a story filled star-crossed love, a le fate itself.

And when the skies and thunder, it will reveal the monster in us all.

The reader has been warned.

Frankenstein's Children

Read the entire haunting trilogy — if you dare . . .

BOOK ONE
The Creation

BOOK TWO
The Revenge

BOOK THREE
The Curse

The FRANKENSTEIN'S CHILDREN Series
by Richard Pierce

THE CREATION
THE REVENGE
THE CURSE

FRANKENSTEIN'S CHILDREN

Book Three:

THE CURSE

Richard Pierce

BERKLEY BOOKS, NEW YORK

FRANKENSTEIN'S CHILDREN: THE CURSE

A Berkley Book / published by arrangement with
the author

PRINTING HISTORY
Berkley edition / January 1995

ISBN: 0-425-14528-X

BERKLEY®
Berkley Books are published by The Berkley Publishing Group,
200 Madison Avenue, New York, New York 10016.
BERKLEY and the "B" design
are trademarks belonging to Berkley Publishing Corporation.

PRINTED IN THE UNITED STATES OF AMERICA

10 9 8 7 6 5 4 3 2 1

For Clint Colker,
who showed me that long-forgotten dreams
can come back to life.
My eternal thanks.

Contents

Something in the Blood

From the diary of Sara Watkins . . .

Some people think love is a chemical thing—a natural force that flows like blood through our veins. No matter how hard we fight it, we can never escape its all-consuming embrace . . .

This I know. Because love was the driving force behind my greatest sin: the resurrection of my dead boyfriend. As I stitched together his broken body, I knew it would end in tragedy. But I couldn't stop myself. I was in love.

Now I've unleashed a nightmare upon the world. And I've discovered that evil is like love. It's something natural, something inescapable . . .

Something in the blood.

Sara Watkins squinted her eyes and searched for a vein in her own forearm. Then, squeezing her left fist until the blood vessels bulged, she reached out with her right hand—and picked up a hypodermic needle.

"I can't look," said Jessie Frank, covering her face with her hands. "I hate the sight of blood."

Sara ignored her. She focused her attention on a

single vein and pressed the point of the needle to her own skin. She paused.

Just do it, she told herself.

Closing her eyes and taking a deep breath, she listened to the sounds inside the old mill. She could hear the water of Thunder Lake gently lapping against the dock—and the softly trickling overflow that turned the paddles of the giant waterwheel.

It reminded Sara of the blood that flowed through her own veins—the blood she was about to extract from her arm.

She opened her eyes and looked over at Jessie. The fourteen-year-old girl was sitting in a corner next to the lab supplies they'd stolen—and her small, round face was buried in her hands. Sara had to laugh. Jessie looked so cute with her short dark hair bunched up around her fingers and her tennis shoes kicking back and forth. Jessie's dog, a big black hound named Baskerville, was lying on the floor next to her, watching Jessie's feet swing dangerously close to his nose.

Do it now, Sara told herself, while Jessie's not looking.

Gritting her teeth, she pushed the hypodermic needle into her arm. She felt the cold steel point penetrate her skin—but she didn't flinch. Not because it didn't hurt. It hurt plenty. But Sara was determined to hide her pain from Jessie . . .

Because it was Jessie's turn next.

Sara pulled back on the tiny plunger, and a thick flow of blood began to fill the chamber of the hypo. Sara bit her lip and waited.

Her eyes seemed to turn a deeper shade of blue

as she focused on the grisly task, and her seventeen-year-old face took on the expression of an older and wiser woman. She could feel the sweat beading up on her forehead, trickling down a strand of her long blond hair.

I must look like a nervous wreck, she thought. Good thing Jessie has her eyes shut.

She stared anxiously at the steady flow of her own blood into the hypodermic. Then, when the chamber was finally full, Sara removed the needle.

"I'm finished," she said. "You can open your eyes now, you big baby."

Jessie dropped her hands to her sides and watched Sara swab the puncture mark with cotton. "I don't get it, Sara. Why take samples of *your* blood? *I'm* the one with monster blood in my veins."

Sara fumbled with a plastic bandage. "I need to compare our samples side by side . . . just to see if your blood is normal."

Jessie smirked. "And you're normal? Give me a break, Sara. You sliced up body parts in the morgue and stitched them onto my dead brother. Now you're sticking needles in yourself and telling me that *you're* normal."

Sara smiled. "Well, my *blood* is normal. I never said anything about my brain."

"Admit it, girl, you're twisted."

"I'm a scientist."

"A *mad* scientist."

The two girls laughed, and the sound echoed in the highest rafters of the old mill.

It felt strange to laugh again—especially here, in

the makeshift laboratory where Sara resurrected her own boyfriend, Jessie's brother.

Josh . . .

Sara's eyes filled with tears. She looked up at the steel chains hanging from the watchtower and remembered the lightning storm that had brought Josh's corpse back to life. Then she studied the slow-turning gears of the mill's waterwheel . . .

"I don't like it here," Jessie blurted out, glancing at the wooden gears. "Every time that waterwheel turns, I think about my mom and dad . . . and how they died."

Sara didn't know what to say.

Jessie pushed a short lock of hair out of her eyes and stared down at the floor. "I see them in my dreams, Sara," she whispered. "Two monsters . . . crawling out of the grave. My own flesh and blood . . . gray and rotted and . . . and covered with worms . . ."

She started to cry. Sara jumped up and crossed the dusty room, her arms reaching out to her best friend. "It's alright, Jessie," she whispered, stroking the girl's hair.

"It's not alright," Jessie gasped, her feet swinging nervously beneath the chair. "My parents were monsters! Grandfather Frank built them out of dead body parts! And I'm their daughter! I don't even know if I'm *human* or not . . . I don't know if I'm alive . . . or if I'm dead . . ."

"You're alive, Jessie. You're alive and kicking."

Jessie lifted her head and wiped the tears from her eyes. "Well, I feel like a zombie," she sighed. "I don't know why I'm still living. Everyone I've ever loved is dead. Josh killed himself. Grandfather Frank fell from the tower window. My boyfriend drowned in the lake. And my parents were ground up by a waterwheel . . ."

There was bitter sarcasm in Jessie's voice as she listed off the horrors like a stand-up comedian. But it was all just an act. She couldn't hide the pain in her heart.

Suddenly, without warning, Jessie burst into tears again.

Sara felt helpless. It was all so horrible and unfair. Jessie was just a kid—a high school freshman who should have been worrying about boys and hair-styles . . . not death and resurrection. But life had brought Jessie nothing but misery. She was innocent, a victim of cruel fate . . .

She was the last of the Frankensteins.

Jessie clenched her fists and cried. "Even my dog . . . even Baskerville . . . is a walking carcass."

Hearing his name, the huge black hound lifted his nose in the air and barked. Then he jumped up with his front paws on Jessie's lap—and licked her face.

"Oh, Baskerville, baby, I'm sorry," said Jessie with a sad smile. "You're not a walking carcass. You're a cyberdog, okay?" She scratched the hound's ears and stroked the electrical bolts in his neck. "You're Robo-pooch."

Baskerville wagged his tail, and Sara laughed.

Then a shadow of gloom crossed over Jessie's face. "Seriously, Sara, I don't like it here," she said. "I keep seeing my mother and father, screaming and dying on that waterwheel . . . It freaks me out. I think I'm losing my mind or something."

Sara frowned. "Well, roll up your sleeve. Let's get this over with."

Jessie closed her eyes and groaned. "Why don't you take a sample of Baskerville's blood? I'm not the only monster around here."

"You're not a monster, Jessie. And anyway, I've already taken a sample of Baskerville's blood. I do it twice a week, just to check for signs of decay."

"Decay?" Jessie felt her heart pounding in her chest. "Do you think I'm going to decay . . . like Josh did . . . before he killed himself?"

Sara bit her lip. All the grisly details of Josh's final days came rushing into her head at once—the uncontrollable rage, the monstrous urges, the rotting flesh . . .

It was all so horribly tragic. Josh had killed himself to avoid turning into a monster. And Sara, in her ignorance and passion, had brought him back to life again.

Forgive me, Josh . . .

Jessie leaned forward in her chair. "Here's how I see it, Sara. Josh is my brother. Our parents were man-made monsters. And if Josh turned into a monster, then I will, too."

Sara shook her head. "We don't know that for a fact, Jessie. I'm a scientist. I need facts. Cold, hard facts." She picked up a hypodermic needle, then turned around and faced her friend.

Jessie cringed. "It's a waste of time, Sara. I'm cursed, I'm doomed, I'm . . ."

"Shut your mouth and roll up your sleeve."

Drop by drop, the water of Thunder Lake turned the wooden paddles of the waterwheel. And drop by drop, the blood of Sara, Jessie, and Baskerville stained the glass of microscope slides. Each drop was tested, analyzed, and examined with a scientific eye. And each cell of blood told a story of its own . . .

"Well?" said Jessie. "Am I going to rot away like a vegetable or what?"

Sara raised her eyes from the microscope. "You and I have the exact same blood type," she said, hesitating.

Jessie's eyes lit up. "So I'm normal, right? Just like you?"

Sara sighed. "Not exactly."

Jessie's smile disappeared. She closed her eyes and fell back against her chair, preparing for the worst. "Go on," she said grimly. "Give me the bad news, doctor."

Sara cleared her throat.

How do I tell her? How do I tell Jessie that her blood is the strangest stuff I've ever seen?

When Sara spoke, her voice quavered. "We're both B Positive blood types," she said, pausing. "But that's where the resemblance ends."

"What do you mean?" Jessie felt something catch in her throat.

"Come take a look." Sara pushed the microscope in

front of Jessie and placed another slide on the platform. Jessie leaned forward and stared into the eyepiece. "This is *my* blood sample," said Sara. "Notice the shape and color of the cells." Jessie nodded. Then Sara replaced the slide with another. "Now take a look at *your* blood sample."

Jessie squinted. "Some of the cells are shaped funny," she whispered. "Why are some of them black?"

Sara didn't answer. She switched the slide with yet another. "This is a sample of Baskerville's blood."

Jessie peered into the microscope—and gasped . . .

Because *all* of the cells were black and oddly shaped.

A cold wave of terror swept through Jessie's body—as dark and real as the blood that flowed through her veins.

"Does this mean . . ."

"It's inconclusive," Sara interrupted. "I need to do more tests before I know . . ."

"You know very well what it means, Sara."

Sara pulled the microscope away from Jessie. "No! I need to run the data through a computer. I need to do some more research . . ."

"You need to face the facts, Sara."

Sara pounded her fist on the table and buried her head in her arms. Her long blond hair spilled across the tabletop, covering the pages of her notes. Frustration and rage surged through her body and soul. Her mind was reeling with horror. And when she finally lifted her head, her eyes were filled with tears.

"I'm sorry, Jessie," she whispered.

The old mill was silent—except for the endless

grinding of the waterwheel. Jessie reached for Sara's hand across the table. She held it tightly.

"You don't have to lie to me, Sara," she said. "You don't have to protect me from the truth. I can figure it out for myself."

A single tear rolled down Sara's face. She loved Jessie so much, she couldn't stand the thought of watching her fall apart . . . day after day . . . rotting away . . .

Like Josh.

"I'm not quite alive and I'm not quite dead," Jessie said slowly, without a trace of emotion. "I'm somewhere in between. I guess it's just a matter of time . . ."

"No!"

Sara jumped up from her chair and started to pace the room. "There's got to be *something* I can do. Some way I can save you. Grandfather Frank said he solved the problem of decay when we reanimated Josh. He said that Josh wouldn't rot. Maybe we can infuse the artificial blood into you, too."

"And turn me into a monster?"

Sara stopped in her tracks and thought about it. "You're right. It would probably kill you . . . unless, of course, we bring you back to life."

Jessie shook her head. "Are you crazy, girl? Baskerville is the only creature you resurrected with any success. It worked on a dog, but it turned your boyfriend into a maniac. And anyway, I'd look terrible in neck bolts."

Sara frowned. "You're right, it's a stupid idea," she sighed. "But I'm not going to give up, Jessie. I'm not going to sit back and watch you die. I'm going to save you. If it's the last thing I do, I'm going to save you!"

Jessie scoffed. "The same way you saved Josh?"

Sara froze, stung by Jessie's words. Tears welled up in her eyes.

Jessie felt like kicking herself. She jumped up and wrapped her arms around Sara. "I'm sorry, Sara, I'm an idiot. I didn't mean to say that," she whispered. "I know how much you loved Josh. You wanted to bring him back. And I helped you do it. It's not your fault, Sara. You did the best you could."

Sara looked at Jessie through a blur of tears— and remembered every detail of the nightmare they had shared. Discovering Josh after the suicide. Stealing lab equipment from the school and body parts from the morgue. Raising the dead in a blaze of lightning . . .

They had been through so much together. Even if it all ended in death.

Sara took a deep breath. "I want to help you, Jessie," she whispered. "That's all. I want to help you."

Jessie wiped a tear from her face. "Well, you'd be a sad excuse for a friend if you didn't."

Sara smiled.

The two girls hugged.

And there, in the old mill on the edge of the lake, the forces of nature were about to be challenged again. Not by the creation of life, but by the destruction of something dark, something evil . . .

Something in the blood of Frankenstein.

2

Cages of the Soul

From the diary of Sara Watkins . . .

As I plunged myself into the mysteries of flesh and blood, I realized that every human soul is born in a cage. We are all prisoners—of our families, our cultures, our bodies and our minds. These are just a few of the cages constructed by the hands of fate. We do not choose them for ourselves. But we are trapped inside them from the day we're born.

Our souls are like birds. We flutter against the bars, beating our wings, longing to fly . . .

The question is: can the cage be broken?

Will we ever fly free?

The creature stirred.

Its first movements were painful, its arms and neck still swollen and tender from the fresh stitches in its skin. Its massive body was laced with scars. And its stone-gray face was a mask of silent suffering—and death.

Slowly, the creature opened its eyes, gazing coldly up at the ceiling . . .

Bars. Steel bars.

The creature was in a cage. Again.

The creature knew this cage. It was hidden beneath the ground, in the cellar of an old mansion. The mansion was the creature's home. Or it used to be. When the creature was still alive.

Alive . . .

It tried to lift its head, but the pain was unbearable. Its body was tightly wrapped in bandages. Somehow, it had been hurt, but it couldn't remember how.

There were clouds in the creature's brain. Huge, dark rain clouds filled with thunder and lightning. A storm was brewing inside its head. And every thought was painful . . .

Who am I?

The question surged through its body like a bolt of electricity, lighting up the darkest corners of its soul. The creature tried to move its long fingers, its massive arms and legs—and was struck by a horrible truth . . .

The limbs belonged to someone else.

They had been sewn onto its body, piece by piece, and sparked with life. Even its head had been opened up, its brain repaired with needle and thread. It was no longer human. The blood that flowed through its veins was not red and warm. The power that surged through its flesh was not a human life force. It was something raw and dangerous. Like lightning.

The creature closed its eyes and searched deep within its soul for an answer. Two words flashed through its mind. Two terrible, frightening words . . .

I'm dead.

And in one powerful rush, a dam burst inside its

brain, flooding its mind with horrible memories . . .

It was human once. A boy. And this boy was turning into a monster because his parents were monsters. His flesh was rotting. His mind was breaking apart. So he jumped from the tower window of the mansion and killed himself.

But it didn't end there. An old man—the boy's grandfather—helped to bring him back to life.

And now he was a monster. Ugly. Grotesque. *Dead* . . .

The creature's vision began to blur. The bars of the cage seemed to bend and sway every time the creature blinked its eyes.

The creature was crying—and the memories kept flowing with its tears . . .

He remembered his mother and father, two savage monsters that he had killed with his own hands. And he remembered Grandfather falling from the mansion tower. They were all dead now. But not him. He was a creature who *lived* in death.

But not true death. That was the one thing the creature wanted most of all. Sweet, merciful death. There was nothing else to live for.

Slowly, the creature turned its head, the tears spilling over the scars on its face. One of its steel neck bolts scraped against the stone floor. Its eyes focused on something in the corner, something made of wood and strings . . .

It was a guitar.

Music . . .

The creature closed its eyes and listened. Deep in its brain was a memory of music. Guitar music. *His* music. Music he used to play when he was alive. Love songs he wrote—for her.

Sara . . .

Yes, the creature remembered. Remembered her face, her eyes, her lips.

Sara . . .

And the creature remembered when there was a reason to live. It was something called *love* . . .

A sudden jolt of pain surged through its limbs. The creature opened its mouth to cry out—but it couldn't. The storm clouds were filling its brain again. Big, black clouds and thunder and lightning. The bars of the cage were fading behind a dark wall of rain. Everything was disappearing . . .

Am I dying?

The creature closed its eyes.

And prayed for death.

"Look at him," said Eddie Perez, pointing through the bars. "He's a zombie. Pardon the expression."

Sara gave her friend a dirty look and stared at the creature on the floor of the cage. "I think he's still in a coma," she said. "He suffered quite a shock, after all. How do you think *you'd* feel after you killed your own parents?"

Eddie shrugged in a gawky, boyish way, his long black hair tumbling over his eyes. "If I killed my parents, they'd come back to haunt me for wrecking the car."

"Are they still mad at you?"

Eddie smirked. "I've been grounded for the rest of my life."

Sara shook her head. Then she crouched down to take a closer look at Josh.

His huge body was sprawled across the floor of the cage, covered with bloodstained bandages. His chest rose and fell in a slow steady rhythm, and his thick, gray eyelids were sealed shut.

And his face . . .

Sara could hardly stand to look at him. Every time she gazed at those sunken cheeks, those broken scars, those wretched stitches—her heart was overwhelmed with emotions. Love. Fear. Revulsion. Guilt. She wished she had never listened to Grandfather Frank. She wished she had never agreed to bring Josh back to life.

Why did I do it? she wondered.

She had seen the head in the freezer—the hideous, dismembered head of the original Frankenstein monster. Now, looking down at Josh's grotesque body and face, she understood that history had repeated itself.

At least his eyes are closed, she thought.

The most disturbing thing of all were those cold dead orbs, staring out through blackened sockets, glowing with eerie, unnatural life . . .

Sara glanced down at the Frank family ring on her finger—the ring Josh gave her on the night he killed himself—and her eyes filled with tears.

Forgive me, Josh.

Sara reached through the bars of the cage. Peeling a bandage from Josh's wrist, she examined the stitches and felt his pulse.

"What's the verdict?" asked Eddie.

Sara shrugged. "He's doing fine. The stitches are healing and his pulse is strong." She paused. "But I'm worried about him. He doesn't respond to anything. He should have snapped out of his coma by now."

She stood up and sighed.

Eddie put his hand on her shoulder. It broke his heart to see Sara like this. Tired. Frustrated. Defeated. He had helped her through every step of Josh's resurrection—and he'd never seen her so beaten.

"You're too hard on yourself, Sara," he said. "Just because you're a scientist doesn't mean you can cure every problem in the world."

Sara pulled herself away from Eddie and walked around the edge of the cage. "I don't think I'm capable of curing anything," she said in a low voice. "Just ask Jessie."

Eddie nodded. "How's it going with her?"

Sara looked up with tears in her eyes. "She's upstairs crying, and I don't blame her. I said I could help her, cure her somehow. But I don't know. I've gone through my dad's entire medical library, and it's useless. Jessie's blood is different than anything ever recorded."

Eddie stuck his hands in his pockets and took a deep breath. "Maybe we should take her to a doctor, Sara."

Sara looked down at the floor. "I know," she whispered. "I mentioned it to Jessie, but she said no."

Eddie tilted his head. "Why not?"

"Think about it, Eddie. The doctors will ask questions. They may want to speak to her legal guardian. And in case you forgot, Grandfather Frank is dead."

Sara pointed to the giant chrome door in the next room. "He's right there in the freezer!"

A chill ran up Eddie's spine. He hated walking past that freezer. It felt . . . haunted, or something.

Sara paced the room, circling the cage nervously. "Can you imagine what would happen if people came snooping around this place? They'd find an old man's corpse in the freezer, the head of the original Frankenstein monster in a block of ice, and a teenage zombie in a cage!"

Sara stopped to catch her breath. She looked up into Eddie's eyes—so dark and beautiful—and somehow, she felt calmer. She didn't know why. It had to be Eddie. Over the past nine weeks, he had helped her through this nightmare. And in the process, he had transformed himself from a geeky computer nerd to a totally cool guy with long hair. Sara looked at him now, amazed at how much he had changed . . .

Or maybe my feelings for him have changed.

"I'm sorry, Eddie," she said. "I guess I'm a little tense."

Eddie walked up to her and began to massage her neck. "You're tired, that's all," he said.

Sara closed her eyes and surrendered to the soothing effects of Eddie's fingers on her neck.

"You just need to relax," he whispered. "You're trying too hard. You're attempting the impossible."

Sara's eyes popped open. "It's not impossible. Nothing is impossible."

Eddie cleared his throat. "Look, Sara," he said, hesitating. "There's something I've been meaning to say. About Josh."

"What about Josh?"

Eddie's hands rested on her shoulders. "I don't think he's in a coma," he whispered. "I think his brain has been damaged."

Sara stared through the bars of the cage. It was painful to see Josh like this. Broken. Wounded. Lifeless. He was the love of her life—and now he was a mockery of death.

"I think his brain was damaged when he killed himself," Eddie went on. "You tried to repair it. But he's never been the same."

Sara couldn't speak. She couldn't deny Eddie's words.

"His brain seemed to fall apart when he fought his mother and father at the mill," said Eddie. "Something happened to him that night. Maybe, during the fight, something snapped. A circuit broke, or his brain tissue was damaged."

Sara's heart was breaking. And when she turned around to face Eddie, she began to cry.

"You're probably right, Eddie," she said. "I'm fighting a losing battle. But how can I let that stop me? How can I give up on Josh and Jessie? I love them, Eddie. And I've got to at least *pretend* that I can save them. How else can I go on living? If they die, what's left for me? Nothing. I'll have nothing to live for."

She burst into tears and leaned against Eddie, sobbing into his chest. With trembling hands, he reached up and stroked her long blond hair.

"You'll always have me, Sara," he whispered.

Sara bit her lip, the hot tears stinging her eyes. There were so many feelings rushing through her, so many emotions, she could barely speak.

"I know," she said. "I love you, Eddie. I really do."

"But . . ."

Sara tried to smile. She knew that Eddie loved her as much as Josh did. But it was too soon. Too soon after the suicide, the resurrection, the never-ending nightmare of life and death . . .

She opened her mouth to explain, but Eddie put a finger to her lips. "Don't say anything," he said. "You know I understand."

Sara nodded.

And kissed him.

For a brief moment, there was a clearing in the storm. The clouds parted, the rain faded to a soft drizzle . . .

And the creature opened its eyes.

At first, it thought it was dreaming. But no. The vision was real. The girl with the yellow hair had come to him at last.

Sara . . .

She was here in the room, on the other side of the cage, just beyond the creature's grasp.

And she was kissing that boy.

A terrible sadness gripped the creature's heart—a feeling even stronger than the desire for death. It wasn't the first time the creature saw the boy kiss the girl with yellow hair. When it happened before, the creature tried to kill the boy, tried to strangle him through the bars of the cage.

But now the creature did nothing.

Because it knew that the world was different outside the cage. It was the world of the living. And the creature did not belong there.

The creature belonged in its cage.

The boy and the girl were leaving now. They didn't even glance at the thing in the cage as they crossed the room and closed the door behind them.

Now the creature was alone.

Like always.

Like it should be.

Not dead, not alive, but alone.

A single tear rolled down the creature's face. Then slowly, painfully, it raised its arm into the air, groping, reaching for the bars of the cage. Its fingers stretched and grasped at nothing.

The bars were so far away.

And then the clouds began to roll across the creature's brain. Thunder filled its ears and lightning blinded its senses.

And as the storm descended upon its mind, the creature opened its gray parched lips and uttered a sound from the loneliest depths of its soul . . .

"*Sa . . . ra.*"

3

And the Dead Shall Rise

From the secret journal of Professor Frank, one hour before his death . . .

Soon I will die at the hands of my own creation.

Josh is coming for me now, coming for revenge. But I am not afraid. I will greet my fate with open arms, knowing that the Frankenstein legacy can never be destroyed. My creations may despise me, curse me, even try to kill me. But the secrets of life and death are eternal. The key to the ultimate mystery shall be mine forever.

Soon, on the first stormy night after my death, the heavens shall open up. The skies will be filled with lightning and thunder . . .

And the dead shall rise.

The town of Thunder Lake, Pennsylvania, was sleeping. Every window was dark and silent; every man, woman, and child, lost in their dreams . . .

But the wind did not sleep. It raced across the black waters of the lake like a frightened animal being stalked by a nightmare. And that nightmare was rising up behind the mountains, rumbling and roaring in the clouds. Its fingers reached out for the wind and grabbed it by the tail. And together, locked in battle, they descended upon the town.

And all hell broke loose.

The storm began with a single deafening crash of thunder. A slash of lightning illuminated the skies, its cold white blade lunging and stabbing at the trembling shadows of houses and trees. Then the rain fell from the skies, its icy needles like salt in the wounds of the earth.

It was a cruel storm, a savage storm. A storm that could raise the dead.

First, it unleashed its fury upon the lake. It attacked the churning waters with glee, torturing the mirrored surface until violent waves crashed against the walls of the concrete dam. Then, seeing that the dam would not break under its force, the storm moved on.

The town was its next victim—a tiny cluster of houses and buildings and tree-lined streets. The storm swept over the town with a single blaze of lightning, exposing the rain-slicked rooftops in one blinding moment. An electrical knife reached down from the clouds and struck a steel lightning rod on the four-story schoolhouse. But it, too, like the dam, would not yield.

Then the storm found a new target . . .

A house on the farthest edge of Thunder Lake—a lonely gray mansion with a black, sagging roof and a tall, pointed tower. It was an old house, a cursed house, a house haunted by the specter of death . . .

It was the House of Frankenstein.

And somehow, it seemed to be calling out to the

storm. Whispering. Beckoning . . .

Come to me.

The storm could not resist. Some unearthly force was pulling it closer and closer to the house, like a magnet. Something deep inside the mansion's walls thirsted for the storm's power—something hungry for the sharp, bitter taste of lightning.

Come to me.

And like a predator drawn to easy prey, the storm descended upon the old, dark house. It raised a jagged claw of lightning high in the air above the rooftop.

Then it reached down—and embraced the tower.

Jessie Frank shifted in her sleep, tossing her head from side to side on the pillow. She was dreaming when the lightning struck the tower, shaking the house from top to bottom.

And her dreams turned into nightmares . . .

She was standing in Thunder Lake Cemetery, looking down at the gravestones of her family and friends.

First, she laid flowers on the graves of Moose and Mike Morgan—two high school boys who were murdered at the hands of monsters. Tears of sadness came to her eyes as she remembered the time when Mike Morgan kissed her. But her tears turned bitter as she recalled how his kisses became too strong, too forceful—only moments before he was killed.

Then, she found herself in front of her family plot. There were three gravestones now. One for Grandfather Frank, one for her brother Josh, and one for her parents. Bending down with a handful of flowers, she whispered a silent prayer . . .

Please forgive them.

But in her heart, she knew that their souls could never be saved.

She reached down to place the flowers on a grave—and something grabbed her hand . . .

Jessie screamed. She looked down in horror and saw the withered hand of Grandfather Frank rising up from the earth, a rotting skeletal claw that held her like a vise, squeezing and pulling her down. She screamed again and tugged against the clutching fingers with all her might. And that's when Josh's massive hand exploded through the dirt, grabbing her other arm . . .

She struggled in vain, crying out in terror. Then the voices of the dead began to echo in her brain.

Join us, Jessie.

She screamed. And fought for her life.

But it was useless. The hands of the dead were too strong, too powerful. And when she tried to dig her feet into the dirt, the gruesome, rotted hands of her parents burst through the earth and closed around her ankles.

Join us, Jessie.

Her brother, her grandfather, her parents—they held her down against the graves, kicking and screaming. Their razor-sharp fingernails dug into her skin. Their horrible voices rang inside her head. But the worst thing of all was the sinking feeling that she could never escape.

She belonged to them now . . .

She was a Frankenstein.

Then, with a sickening sense of dread, Jessie realized what her family was doing—they were pulling her down into the earth . . .

Join us, Jessie.

She tried to scream, but her mouth was filled with dirt. Her arms and legs disappeared into the graves, her body swallowed up by the earth. She felt herself sinking deeper and deeper. The world of the living disappeared above her as the arms of the dead embraced her from below.

Then everything was darkness . . .

And Jessie woke up.

At first, she thought she was still dreaming—because the house was engulfed by lightning. The light in her bedroom was almost blinding. A surge of electricity filled the air.

Jessie swore she could feel it inside her, boiling her blood, sparking every cell of her body with unnatural life. It was almost as if the lightning was unleashing something dark and powerful deep within her.

You're crazy, Jess, she told herself. It's just a lightning storm.

Then she lay back against her pillow, closed her eyes and tried to sleep. But she couldn't. The storm was raging outside her bedroom window—and her entire body was pulsating with energy.

It flashed through her mind that something horrible was happening to her, changing her forever . . .

And she was right.

The storm swirled and embraced the house, basking in the glory of its accomplishment. Its long fingers

of lightning had pierced the cracked walls—and penetrated the flesh of a small human girl. The storm had
never felt so strong or so radiant.

But there was more work to be done.

There were other vessels waiting in the house, waiting to be filled. There, in the lowest depths of the
house, something yearned for its power, its thunder,
its lightning . . .

How could the storm resist?

The creature opened its eyes.

But the dreams of lightning and thunder did not
go away. Even locked in its cage in the basement
of the house, the creature seemed to understand what
was happening. The storm wasn't in its head anymore . . .

The storm was real.

Invisible waves of electricity surged through the
room and crashed against the dull gray pores of the
creature's skin. The vibrating current flowed into its
body through each broken scar, every torn stitch, even
through its ears and mouth and eyes . . .

The creature struggled against the attack. It turned
its massive head from side to side, crying out in pain.

"Sa . . . ra!"

But the creature cried in vain. Nothing could stop
a force as powerful as nature itself. The wind howled
in triumph. The rain pounded against the sides of
the house. And then, in a blazing crash of thunder
and lightning, the storm invaded every cell of the
creature's hideous form.

It was the spark of life itself.

And it was the creature's curse.

He could feel his mind again, coming alive with each jolt of electricity. It made him feel human. Which, of course, made him feel pain.

He could even remember his own name . . .

Josh.

And then the creature began to cry, his eyes burning from the hot salty tears of love and hate, joy and sorrow, misery and grief.

These were the tears of life—a life he never wanted.

A life that never seemed to end.

Suddenly, another loud crash of thunder shook the entire mansion—and a violent jolt swept through the creature's body and soul. His huge, muscled arms shot up into the air, wracked with spasms. His heavy, powerful legs kicked against the floor.

Crawling to the edge of the cage, groaning in pain, the creature lifted his body up and clung to the bars. Then, slowly, he pulled himself up until he was standing, his head grazing the top of the cage.

And he knew it was hopeless. He was doomed. He was cursed . . .

He was alive.

The storm roared in victory. Every electron of its being had penetrated the house, filling every corner and crevice with the sound and fury of nature . . .

But wait.

What was that? In the basement. A door made of steel.

The storm reached down with a finger of lightning and probed the mansion's walls . . .

Yes, there.

It was a tiny crack in the stone foundation of the house, just big enough for a single needle of electricity. The storm rumbled with excitement—and explored the small room behind the steel door . . .

What's this?

The little room was so cold. Like ice. Like the frozen ends of the earth that the storm had seen in its travels—empty white places filled with ice and snow. But there was no snow here in the little room. There was something else . . .

The lifeless body of an old man.

And the head of a strange creature inside a block of ice.

Normally the storm would not bother with such things. They were dead things. No fun at all. But the storm was still glowing from its earlier triumphs— and was somehow drawn to these cold dead things. So, reaching out with a shimmering finger, it pierced a hole in the block of ice . . .

And touched the frozen head of the Frankenstein monster.

At first, nothing happened. Then, in a blinding crackle of sparks, the creature's eyes blazed with life. The rotting flesh twitched across its fractured skull like a swarming sea of maggots, and blue-black drops of artificial blood began to ooze from its scars.

It was a hideous sight to behold—the dismembered head of a man-made creature coming to life after two hundred years. Two hundred years of torment.

Two hundred years of anger. Two hundred years of hunger.

The creature's glowing eyes rolled in their sockets like two red-hot coals. Then, grinding its massive gray jaw, the nightmare opened its mouth . . .

And began to eat its way through the ice.

The storm could taste the creature's fury—and hungered for more. More flesh. More blood. More life. So it turned its attention to the thing on the floor of the basement freezer . . .

The old man.

His body was thin and bent and covered with blood, his crushed legs twisted beneath his torso. His gnarled hands were laced with scars. And his head hung sideways from a broken spine. He had suffered a violent death—falling from the highest tower of the mansion to the hard stone path below. Death, for him, was cruel but swift.

The storm, however, promised to be kind.

A thin bolt of lightning flared out into a trembling claw of electricity. Like a gentle nursemaid, it stroked the old man's neck and legs. Slowly. Lovingly. Then, feeling no response, it dug its nails in deeper, piercing the skin, probing his veins, his nerves, his spinal cord . . .

Until the old man danced on the floor like a broken puppet.

And opened his eyes.

Grandfather Frank was alive. Again.

His first sensation was one of pain—shooting through his limbs like a million needles, touching every cell of his body. But to a man who has been trapped in death, any human feeling—even pain—is a thing of joy . . .

Grandfather Frank began to laugh.

"I'm alive. Alive!"

And his laughter filled the small dark freezer as he pulled himself up on his shattered legs, his joy overwhelming his agony. His head lolled from side to side on his fractured neck. Blood streamed down his chest, his arms, his legs . . .

But still he laughed.

Because he was alive. Alive for a purpose. His heart overflowed with emotion, his mind spinning out of control. There was so much to do. So much to create. And so much to destroy.

He leaned against the huge chrome door of the freezer and laughed again. Touching the wounds on his body, he made a quick mental list of all the repairs that needed to be done—bone mending, organ transplants, surgical stitches. He wasn't worried about his injuries. It was all just simple patchwork—compared to the master plan brewing inside his head . . .

A plan that would restore honor and pride to the noble name of Frankenstein.

It was brilliant. It was inspired.

And it was insane.

Because Grandfather Frank's head had been crushed in the fatal fall.

Still, he retained most of his scientific knowledge and basic functions. He could walk, talk, see, hear . . .

And what he heard inside that dark basement freezer was the sound of gnashing teeth. The old man tilted his fractured head and listened carefully. There it was again—the sound of someone chewing on ice. He reached up and turned on the light inside the freezer. And when he saw the head of the original monster, glaring at him from the shelf, Grandfather Frank began to laugh again.

"Oh, my, look at you! I guess I'm not the only one who loves a stormy night."

The gruesome thing stared back at Grandfather Frank with cold, dark hatred. It bared its yellow teeth like a snarling dog and snapped its jaws.

"Still mad at the world after all these years?" said Grandfather Frank. "Well, no point in losing your head over it."

The old man reached up and grabbed the creature by the hair. It tried to bite him, but Grandfather Frank was too quick. He held the thing carefully in front of him, then opened the door of the freezer and stepped out.

Josh looked up from his cage and stared at the broken man with cold, blank eyes. Grandfather Frank smiled back at him through a face of dried blood.

"I'll come back for you later, my boy," he said.

Then, swinging the dismembered head by his side, the old man staggered up the basement stairs . . .

And vanished into the night.

4

School Spirits

From the front page of *The Weekly Thunder*, the Thunder Lake High School newspaper . . .

WHO—OR WHAT—IS HAUNTING OUR SCHOOL?
As Thunder Lake High gears up for the big Homecoming game before Thanksgiving, many students wonder if we really need any more "school spirit" than we already have. A different kind of "spirit" seems to be stalking our halls: the supernatural kind. And it has cursed our school with tragedy upon tragedy. First, an unidentified "monster" attacked several students. Then, star quarterback Moose Morgan jumped to his death from the school rooftop. Finally, on the same night the "monster" invaded the Halloween Dance, Moose Morgan's brother Mike drowned in Thunder Lake. Now everyone wants to know . . .
Who—or what—is haunting our school? And how do we stop it?

When the school bell rang, students swarmed into the halls like bees in a hive. Everyone was buzzing about the article in the school paper—and everyone had a theory . . .

"It's the work of a satanic cult."

"I think the school principal is behind it all."

"Maybe Thunder Lake High is the Gateway to Hell."

But only three people knew the truth—Sara Watkins, Eddie Perez, and Jessie Frank—a tormented trio of teens who knew that the curse of Thunder Lake was not a spirit at all, but a living thing of flesh and blood. The only ghosts in the school were the painful memories of Moose and Mike Morgan that haunted their guilty souls.

Sara waited for Eddie and Jessie by the water fountain in the lobby. She leaned against the wall, staring at Moose Morgan's broken football trophy in the display case—and felt a pang of remorse.

She'd never liked Moose. He was mean and obnoxious. But that didn't mean he deserved to die at the hands of the monster she'd created. Now everyone thought he had killed himself for love.

She sighed and hugged her books to her chest.

When is this nightmare going to end? she wondered.

A cluster of students walked by her, chatting about Mike Morgan and how he drowned. "He was murdered," said a tall, red-haired girl. "Jimbo and Crusher said they saw two monsters pull him into the lake."

Sara cringed. Because she knew it was true. The two monsters were Josh and Jessie's parents, risen from the grave. But Jessie told the police a different story.

"Sara!"

She looked up to see Eddie Perez bounding toward her, his long black hair spilling out of a baseball cap. He smiled and nodded like a sweet, awkward puppy as he crossed the lobby and kissed her cheek.

"Hi, Eddie. Why so happy?"

Eddie grinned mysteriously. "I just figured out a way to access the computer files of the Center for Disease Control. Maybe, if we scan through all their stuff, we can find a case similar to Jessie's."

Sara shrugged. "I doubt it," she said grimly. "But thanks a lot. It's worth a try."

Eddie's smile disappeared. "Is something wrong, Sara? You seem gloomier than usual."

Sara turned away from the tall boy and watched the steady flow of high school students in the hall—each of them clutching a copy of *The Weekly Thunder*. "It's that article in the paper," she said. "Who—or what— is haunting our school? Well, I know the answer. It's me. I can't help feeling responsible for the deaths of those boys."

Eddie sighed and touched her arm. "I know," he said. "I feel the same way. But we can't keep blaming ourselves. We didn't know it would end this way. Anyway, there's nothing we can do about it now."

Sara nodded slowly. "That's not the only thing that's bothering me," she said. "I can't get Jessie's problem out of my mind. I couldn't sleep at all last night. I lay in bed, listening to the thunderstorm until dawn . . . and thinking about blood. Jessie's blood. The blood of Frankenstein. I dozed off for a few seconds, but then I started dreaming about blood . . . all of Thunder Lake filled with blood . . . and I was drowning in it."

Eddie saw the tears in Sara's eyes and reached out to comfort her. She fell into his arms, trembling. "I don't know if I can save her," she whispered, weeping softly. "I think I'm going to lose her, too . . . like I've lost Josh." She burst into tears.

Eddie held her, stroking her long blond hair and whispering in her ear, "It's okay, Sara." He felt her heart pounding against his chest and her tears on his neck. And he wished he could hold her forever.

Get a grip, Eddie, he told himself. She's still in love with Josh.

But he couldn't help his feelings. Just once, he wanted to hold her the way a man holds a woman. With love. With passion. Not as a friend offering comfort in a time of tragedy.

Unfortunately, it was tragedy that brought them together. The tragedy of Josh's suicide. And it was his resurrection that kept Sara and Eddie bound in a relationship that couldn't be defined. Not friends, not lovers, but something in between.

"You've got to get a hold of yourself, Sara," he whispered. "And you've got to do it fast."

Sara looked up, confused.

Eddie pointed over her shoulder. "I see Jessie in the hall, and she's heading this way."

"Oh." Sara pulled away from Eddie, wiping the tears from her face. She took a deep breath, tried to smile, and turned to greet her best friend. "Jessie! What's up?"

Jessie looked like a wild beast unleashed. Pushing her way impatiently through a crowd of students, she crossed the lobby in leaps and bounds, descending upon Sara and Eddie like a hungry predator circling its prey. Her short dark hair was a tangled nest, and her eyes burned with silent rage.

Sara had never seen her like this. It was more than just strange. It was terrifying.

"What are you two smiling for?" Jessie snapped. "What's there to smile about?"

Sara was speechless. She glanced at Eddie for help.

"Oh, I, ah, found a way to tap into the Center for Disease Control's computer," Eddie stuttered.

"Yeah," said Sara, picking up his cue. "We might be able to help you by comparing your blood to the diseases in their files."

Jessie sighed and ran her fingers through her hair. "It won't do any good," she muttered. "Can't you see, I'm cursed."

Sara felt her heart skip a beat. "What do you mean, Jessie?"

The wild-haired girl threw her hands in the air. "Just look at me, Sara! I'm a mess! I'm turning into a monster before your very eyes, I know I am. It was that thunderstorm last night!"

Sara took a step closer and spoke softly. "What are you talking about?"

"The thunderstorm! Last night! You must have heard it, unless you're deaf. It woke me up in the middle of the night and . . . and . . ." Tears came to Jessie's eyes as she gasped for air.

Sara put her arm around Jessie's shoulder. "Slow down, Jess. Take a deep breath and relax. Do you want some water?"

"No, I don't want water! What do I look like? A fish?"

Sara glanced at Eddie, her eyes filled with concern. "Calm down, Jessie. We're only trying to help you," she said quietly. "Now take your time . . . and tell us everything about last night."

Jessie sighed, a single tear flowing down her face. She looked down at the floor for a few seconds, then looked up at Sara and Eddie. "I was having a nightmare," she said, softly. "My family was trying to pull me down into their graves. It was . . . horrible. They wanted me to join them. They dragged me down into the earth, deeper and deeper, but I couldn't scream. My mouth was filled with dirt. But then the thunder woke me up. A big loud booming crash of thunder. Suddenly I could scream again . . . and I did."

Jessie paused. Sara squeezed her shoulder. "Go on, Jessie. Then what happened?"

Pushing a wild strand of hair from her eyes, Jessie bit her lip and continued. "I sat up in bed and opened my eyes. But everything was white . . . blinding white . . . as if the whole room was filled with lightning. There was lightning everywhere. Lightning on the floor. Lightning in the ceiling. *Lightning inside of me . . .* "

Sara frowned. "What do you mean?"

Jessie shrugged and squinted her eyes. "I don't know, really. But somehow, I could *feel* the lightning in my body. It was everywhere, I tell you. In my lungs, my heart, my head . . . lightning everywhere . . . flowing through me . . . *changing* me."

"Changing you?"

Jessie closed her eyes and nodded. "Something happened inside my body. I don't know what. Something changed. It felt like my blood was boiling. And my brain was going a mile a minute, all these thoughts rushing through my head at once."

"What kind of thoughts?"

Jessie opened her eyes and gazed coldly at Sara. "Bad thoughts," she said. "Scary thoughts. I didn't know my mind was capable of thoughts like that. When the lightning went away, my brain kept spinning. My body kept shaking. I was still changing, even when the storm moved away."

Sara held her friend's hand. "Maybe it's just a normal reaction to lightning," she said. "It must have struck your house. That could explain it."

Jessie shook her head. "You don't understand, Sara," she said, pulling her hand away. "I still feel it. Right now, as we speak. I can feel myself changing."

Sara didn't know what to say. She had to admit that Jessie *did* look different—older, paler, wilder. And it was definitely *not* the result of one night of bad sleep. She wondered with dread if the electrical storm had unlocked something in Jessie's blood. Something monstrous . . .

"I'll have to take another blood sample," she said, "just to make sure you're not imagining this."

"I'm *not* imagining this," Jessie insisted. "The changes inside of me are as real as . . . as real as Heather Leigh Clark, who's marching right toward us."

Sara and Eddie groaned and turned to look. Sure enough, the bouncy blond cheerleader was parading across the lobby, smiling and waving at them as if they were the best of friends. Which they weren't.

"*Sara! Jessie!* I've been looking *everywhere* for you two!" Heather Leigh Clark grinned from ear to ear. Which made Sara and Jessie very uneasy.

"What do you want, Heather?" Jessie said, flatly.

"I have *great* news for both of you! *Great* news!" She glanced at Eddie with distaste. "Oh, hi, Eddie."

"Hi, Heather."

Sara sighed. "What's the great news?"

The cheerleader smiled and hissed through her teeth. "You're not going to believe it, Sara! You've been nominated for Homecoming Queen!"

Sara's mouth dropped open. "What?"

"It's true, Sara! As a member of the Homecoming committee, I helped count the ballots, and it's definitely for real. You could be our next Homecoming Queen! Isn't it a riot?"

Sara felt numb. "A riot," she muttered.

Eddie couldn't help laughing. "That's great, Sara! I love it! Sara Watkins, Homecoming Queen!"

"Don't count your chickens before they're hatched," Heather interrupted. "After all, she'll be competing with *moi*! And I might add that I was elected *Queen* of the Junior *Prom* last year. So look out, Sara! I'm ready to do *anything* to get that crown!"

Sara shook her head and stared at the floor. "I don't get it," she said. "I'm not the Homecoming Queen type. How did *I* get nominated?"

Heather tilted her head. "Well, between you and me, Sara, I think you impressed everyone with the decorations you did for the Halloween Dance. I mean,

Frankenstein's laboratory! It was *too* much! You really *outdid* yourself!"

"Oh, not really," said Sara.

Jessie almost burst out laughing, but stopped herself. "You said you were looking for me, too?" she said to Heather.

The cheerleader tossed her hair over a shoulder and smiled. "That's right, Jessie. And you're gonna *freak* when I tell you. You're gonna *die*!"

"Just tell me," said Jessie. "I can't bear the suspense."

"*Wellll*," said Heather coyly. "I don't know if you heard, but Maggie Wimmer's family is moving to California next week. Which means we need another freshman cheerleader. So we pulled out our records from last year's tryout and saw that *you* were next in line to be on the squad! So, whattaya say, Jessie? You can be a *cheerleader* now! Isn't that *fabulous*?"

Jessie was speechless.

Sara smiled. "Wow, that's great, Jessie. I can see you now, doing cartwheels in a cute little skirt."

"Yeah, congratulations," said Eddie.

Jessie bit her lip and stared at Heather. "I don't know . . ."

Heather's jaw dropped. "What do you mean, *you don't know*? Are you *crazy*? Most girls would give their right *arm* to be a cheerleader!"

"I know," Jessie mumbled. "It's just . . . with everything that's happened . . . I mean, my brother Josh being so sick . . . I feel funny about doing it. It's not a good time."

"It's the *best* time," said Heather. "When life kicks dirt in your face, you gotta make mud pies!"

Sara put her hand on Jessie's shoulder. "She's right, you know. Maybe it'll be good for you . . . to get your mind off of things."

Jessie stared down at her body—the body she knew was beginning to change. Any day now, she could rot and decay. In a matter of months, she could be dead. Or worse.

"Okay, I'll do it," she whispered.

"All *right*!" Heather clapped her hands and hopped up and down. "Let's *do* it, girl! I'll see you at practice after school!"

Then the blond cheerleader spun around and bounced away.

Sara, Jessie, and Eddie were left dumbstruck. And for a brief moment in time, this tormented trio of teens stopped worrying about life and death and resurrection . . .

And started pondering the mysteries of high school.

5

Six Feet Under

From *The Coal County Daily News* . . .

THUNDER LAKE FIGHTS BACK
*Local Cops Unleash Guard Dogs
on Lovers' Lane and Cemetery*

From *The Weekly Thunder*

THE PARTY'S OVER
*Lovers' Lane and Cemetery Off Limits:
Beware of Dog!!*

From *The Pennsylvania Scandal* . . .

MONSTER MUTTS TERRORIZE TINY TOWN
Are They Canine Cops—or Hounds From Hell?

The moon rose up over Thunder Lake Cemetery like a pale silver ghost ship floating on a midnight sea of gravestones and shadows. All was calm. Even the wind from the lake had settled in for the night, laying a blanket of cold air over the tombs of the dead. Nothing moved, nothing breathed, nothing lived . . .

Except Killer.

Killer was a police dog—a massive, thick-necked rottweiler with short black fur and a hard-muscled body. Every day at six o'clock, when the gates of Thunder Lake Cemetery were closed to the public, Killer went on patrol.

And Killer ruled the night.

Slowly, stealthily, he walked the perimeter of the graveyard. Watching. Listening. If a single leaf fell to the ground, he snarled. If a cricket chirped, he pounced. If a car drove past the cemetery, he hurled himself against the fence and barked madly through the bars.

Because that's how Killer was trained. To guard. To protect. To attack. And Killer took pride in his work. He was a police dog, and he was the best.

But he didn't much like this job.

It was boring, patrolling these lifeless grounds from dusk to dawn. He missed his companions back at the police station. He missed Officer Colker. He missed the warmth of his bed. He missed his dog bowl.

Here, there were no such comforts. Here, among the cold gray stones, there was only death. He could smell it in the air—the sharp aroma of decay rising up from the earth itself. Death, death, and more death . . .

Killer yawned.

He was tired of circling the cemetery, tired of chasing bugs and barking at cars. So he searched for a comfortable place to lie down—which wasn't easy. Many of the graves were old, and the foul odor of rot stung the dog's sensitive nose. At last, he found a spot near the bottom of the hill—two fresh graves covered with a soft layer of dirt. The smell wasn't so bad here. So Killer dug his paws into the earth, sprawled out on his stomach, and closed his eyes.

In thirty seconds, he was fast asleep and dreaming—blissfully unaware of the fact that he was sleeping on the fresh graves of Moose and Mike Morgan.

Six feet under, the dead were dreaming, too.

Beneath the heavy gray tombstones and layers of dark earth lay the bodies of Moose and Mike Morgan. And deep in the folds of their lifeless brains lay the memories of their murders . . .

For death does not destroy human memories. Every thought, every emotion, every event in a person's life is etched into the brain as deeply as the names carved on their headstones. Every wrinkle has a secret, every convolution tells a story.

And every story ends in death.

Moose Morgan's brain was filled with memories of high school, of football stardom, of winning a trophy—and falling in love with Heather Leigh Clark. They were good memories, most of them. Until the night he was killed.

He had taken Heather to Lovers' Lane that night. He wanted to declare his love and offer her his class ring. But the beautiful cheerleader rejected him. She threw his ring in the lake and stomped away. And Moose was left alone. Humiliated. Angry. He walked into the icy waters of the lake to find his class ring. And that's when the nightmare began . . .

A monster—a huge, hideous, disfigured monster—rose up from the water and grabbed him. The creature's powerful hands wrapped around Moose's neck. He thought he was going to die then and there. But Moose managed to break free—and grab the baseball bat in his car. As he swung the bat at the monster's head, Moose was overwhelmed by fear and disgust. He had never seen anything so horrible in his life. The creature's face was laced with stitches, its eyes, so cold and dead.

He wanted to kill it—more than anything in the world, Moose Morgan wanted to watch this monster die.

He chased it through the woods to the high school. He followed it up the stairs to the roof of the building. Suddenly the skies were filled with thunder. Cold needles of rain assaulted them from above. And the battle began.

There, high above the streets of Thunder Lake, Moose and the monster fought like wild animals. Moose was merciless, slamming the bat into the creature's head with all his might. But the monster was stronger . . .

The baseball bat was wrenched from Moose's grip and thrown over the side of the rooftop. The powerful creature lifted Moose up over his head, ready to toss him to his death. And Moose screamed for his life.

He looked down at the four-story drop to the hard concrete below. He prayed for a miracle—and that's when Sara, Jessie, and Eddie showed up.

Moose knew them from school. They weren't really his friends—they were geeks, after all. But when a monster is dangling your body over a rooftop, you're in no position to be picky about your friends.

He screamed for help. Sara shouted out, "Josh, no!" And in one blinding flash, Moose realized that the monster was Joshua Frank—one of his own classmates! But how could that be? The arms that held Moose high in the air were too massive and strong to be Josh's. It seemed as if Josh's body was a patchwork of other human parts. Stitched together. Like Frankenstein.

And that was Moose's last thought—as his body was thrown over the side of the roof.

Frankenstein . . .

He screamed as he fell headfirst toward the street. The concrete swelled up below him. And swallowed him whole.

Now, everything was darkness.

His new home was a mahogany casket, six feet under the earth. And his brother was only a few feet away—dreaming of a life and death that was every bit as horrifying as Moose's . . .

Mike Morgan was basically a good kid. He played the tuba in the marching band. He cracked jokes in the classroom. And he flirted shamelessly with Jessie Frank—which was the biggest mistake of his life. And the last.

It happened on the night of the big Halloween dance. Mike asked Jessie to be his date, wearing his and her mummy costumes. Everything was going great—until Mike talked Jessie into going to Lovers' Lane. They parked the car near the lake. Mike made a move on Jessie. Jessie told him to slow down, but Mike couldn't stop himself. He grabbed her, kissed her, tore at her clothes. Then, in a sudden burst of violence, the car door was wrenched open . . .

And Mike Morgan was dragged out of the car by two half-rotted zombies.

They were creatures born from a nightmare—a man and woman who looked like they'd been buried for decades. Their flesh was rotted away, their bones dry and brittle. But they were strong enough to carry Mike to the edge of the lake—and throw him in the water.

When Mike looked up at the shore and saw the two monsters coming in after him, he started swimming for his life. He splashed desperately in the water, paddling as fast as he could. But they were right behind him. And as soon as he reached the middle of the lake, they caught him . . .

And pulled him down to the bottom.

Even in death, Mike's brain could not fully grasp the final horrible moments of his life. But the memory was burned in forever—struggling in the blackest depths of the lake, gasping for air and swallowing water, trying to scream as the creatures' claws dug into his flesh . . . then feeling his life drain away, drop by drop.

These were the dreams of the dead.

Killer's dreams were also filled with blood. But the blood was dripping off a thick, juicy, raw steak.

The big dog shifted in his sleep, licking his chops and kicking dirt off the graves of the Morgan boys. His jaws opened and closed on his dream steak—

but then reality pulled the steak away. Something in the cemetery made his ears twitch and his nose wriggle . . .

A human presence.

Killer rolled over and opened his eyes. The cemetery was dark and silent. No visible signs of life. Just the smell of something human. His eyes searched the night, his fur standing on end. Nothing. But, wait. There, behind a tall gravestone . . .

Someone was hiding.

The rottweiler crouched down and waited. He bared his fangs. Then, moving slowly from gravestone to gravestone, the predator closed in on his prey.

There was danger in the air, and something evil—Killer could smell it. This was no ordinary human. This human was more ferocious than any attack dog.

Killer knew he had to stay calm and keep his head in control of his animal instincts. Digging his paws into the ground, he fixed his gaze on the human shadow. His eyes zeroed in on the human's throat—which he planned to tear open with his jaws. Then pulling back and baring his teeth, he snarled and jumped . . .

And that's when Killer lost his head.

Six feet under, Moose and Mike Morgan stopped dreaming.

Even in death, they sensed the brutal act of violence that was being committed on top of their own graves. And even in death, they felt the ground above them shift and stir.

Six feet above, a dog yelped in pain. Blood splashed across the gravestones. Then a pair of red-stained hands started digging into the earth . . .

Into the graves of the Morgan brothers.

Their caskets groaned and creaked as handful after handful of mossy dirt was ripped from their tombs. The cold night air seeped into the earth, penetrating the cracks of their mahogany boxes—and piercing the skin of their corpses.

There was nothing the Morgan boys could do to stop it. They had no choice but to wait—patiently, helplessly—as their graves were defiled.

Suddenly, without warning, the lids of their caskets were wrenched open.

The wood splintered and cracked. The moonlight burned like fire on their pale, exposed flesh. And the cruel, blood-drenched hands reached down to claw their bodies, grabbing and tearing, ripping and pulling . . .

Until, one after another, their corpses were lifted up and out of their eternal resting places.

They were tossed like rag dolls over their gravestones, next to the decapitated carcass of a dog. The stench of death filled the air. And laughter, too—cold, evil laughter that echoed across the cemetery.

Then, one by one, the bodies were dragged across the graveyard, over the gates, into the night.

And once again, all was calm in Thunder Lake Cemetery. The moon, like a pale silver ghost ship, sailed across the gravestones of the Morgan brothers—illuminating three simple words carved in stone . . .

Rest in peace.

6

The Sleep of Reason

From the diary of Sara Watkins . . .

Last night, I told Jessie to have sweet dreams.

We made a deal with each other. Before we went to sleep, we'd push the bad thoughts out of our minds and focus on the good. Then we'd close our eyes and drift away to a place where monsters didn't exist. Where Jessie was a cheerleader and I was the Homecoming Queen.

Now it's morning. And the fear in my heart is as strong as the sun streaming through my bedroom window. I realize now that it's hopeless. Even the sweetest dreams can turn into nightmares . . .

The sleep of reason produces monsters.

The red morning sun stained the sky like a drop of blood on a white satin sheet. Its light was cold and merciless, its glaring rays exposing every crack and crevice in the gray peeling walls of the Frank family mansion.

The whole house seemed to cringe in fear. Like a vampire at sunrise.

But the mansion couldn't crawl beneath the earth to

hide in darkness. Instead, it defied the cruel sunlight by raising its tower high and proud—daring the morning rays to shine down and illuminate the Victorian house in all its hideous grandeur.

At exactly seven o'clock, in a small bedroom on the third floor, an alarm clock began to ring. Jessie Frank stirred in her sleep, yawned, stretched . . .

And even before she opened her eyes, she knew something was wrong.

Horribly wrong.

She could smell it in the air—a sharp, dank aroma that filled the room. And she could feel it all over her body—a damp, muddy coating that clung to her skin.

She opened her eyes.

And screamed.

Looking down in shock and horror, she saw her hands, her feet, her pillow and sheets—caked with moist brown earth and wet sticky blood. Her nightshirt was dirty and torn. Her bedroom was in shambles.

"Nooo!"

She cried out in terror and shame—because somehow she knew that *she* was responsible for this.

Jumping out of bed and turning off the alarm, Jessie surveyed the damage in her room. Books had been thrown from the shelves, pages ripped out and strewn across the floor. A tall lamp lay shattered on her desk. And Bessie—her favorite childhood doll—had been torn limb from limb . . .

"Nooo!"

She knelt down and picked up the broken pieces of

her beloved doll. A single tear trickled down Jessie's face.

I'm still dreaming, she told herself. This is not real.

But then she felt the painful sting of cuts and bruises on her arms and legs—and she knew she wasn't dreaming. She studied her wounds. It looked like she'd been running through the woods all night, her body slashed by thorns and branches.

Then Jessie looked at the blood on her sheets.

"Oh, please, please," she whispered to herself. "Let it be my blood . . . my blood alone . . . and nobody else's."

Suddenly her whole body began to tremble violently. She reached for the chair by her desk and collapsed onto the seat. Her head was spinning, her heart pounding. She closed her eyes tightly—and tried to remember her dreams.

At first, it was hard to concentrate. Her mind was reeling in shock. But then she forced herself to relax. And slowly, a dark web of visions unfolded before her . . .

Running. Running through the woods. Like an animal, wild and free. Hunting. You're hunting for food, crawling through the thorns, chasing something. What is it? A squirrel, yes. That's it, a squirrel. Stalking it, chasing it, grabbing its tail and twisting its neck and biting its throat and drinking its blood . . .

"Nooo!"

Jessie opened her eyes. Her hands were shaking, her hair drenched in sweat.

It's just a dream, she told herself.

Then she looked at the blood on her bed, her night-shirt, her hands—and she knew she was lying to herself. This was no dream. It was real. She stood up slowly and crossed the room, then stared into the mirror above her dresser.

Her lips were stained with blood.

Jessie's legs began to tremble again. She glanced down at her feet, caked with mud, and rushed back to her chair before she almost passed out.

Stay cool, Jessie, she told herself. Just close your eyes and concentrate, try to remember everything.

She closed her eyes. And once again, her mind was overwhelmed by dark, confusing images . . .

The woods, the lake. Running, jumping, snarling. Then climbing the gate, a big iron gate, up and over and running again, past tall stones and short stones. Gravestones, that's what they are. And you're running through the cemetery, searching . . . for who? Mother and father? No. Searching for him, searching for Mike Morgan, who kissed you that night, who drowned in the lake, murdered by your monstrous parents. Looking for Mike, finding his grave and digging, digging, digging . . .

Suddenly the vision ended.

And Jessie opened her eyes.

The blinding sunlight poured through the window, drowning her bedroom in a merciless flood of truth. The daylight illuminated her nightmare, every horrible detail—the shattered lamp, the ripped-up books, the broken doll, the muddy, bloody bedspread . . .

Jessie began to sob. She remembered Sara telling her to have sweet dreams—but now Jessie realized that sweet dreams were no longer possible . . .

Only nightmares. Real nightmares. Like suicide, resurrection, and monsters.

Like me . . .

Jessie wept silently. She clenched her fists and took a deep breath. Then she closed her eyes—and listened to the blood flowing through her veins.

It was like music.

It hummed and buzzed through her body, dancing and singing with a life all its own. Her blood soared with the music, waltzing through her arteries, spinning and whirling through her veins. And the pounding of her heart was a symphony . . .

What's happening to me? she wondered.

Unfortunately, she knew the answer . . .

She was turning into a monster. Like her mother, her father, her brother. Because she was cursed.

She was a Frankenstein.

For some strange reason, the thought calmed her down. She stopped crying. She looked at the mess in her room—and the dirt and blood on her body— and she decided to just relax and deal with it.

Taking a deep breath, she walked to the bathroom, undressed, and stepped into the shower. The water was hot and soothing—and it washed everything away . . .

The mud. The dirt. The blood.

She stared down at the floor of the tub, watching the swirling mass of brown and red disappear down the drain. She scrubbed her body with soap—first her hands and face, then her feet and legs. It felt good to get clean, to wash away all the filth and grime and horror . . .

It was almost as if her very soul had been cleansed.

As she stepped out of the shower and dried herself off, Jessie wondered how she would tell Sara about this.

Maybe I should keep it a secret, she thought. I was only sleepwalking, after all.

Then Jessie went back to her bedroom, hardly glancing at the dirty, bloody sheets on her bed. She didn't want to think about it now. She had to get ready for school. She had cheerleading practice today, and she couldn't miss it.

She looked out at the sunshine beaming through her window, and smiled.

It's a beautiful day, she thought.

And then suddenly her eyes were filled with tears again, her stomach all tied up in knots. Her moods were shifting so quickly, so violently, she couldn't control them.

For a second, she was afraid she'd start screaming.

No, she told herself. You're *not* going to scream. You're *not* a monster.

Then she turned on her radio and listened to music as she looked for something to wear. Soon, she was feeling in control again. She even hummed along with the music as she slipped into her clothes.

And then the music stopped.

"We interrupt this broadcast to bring you a special news report from Thunder Lake," said a deeply serious voice.

Jessie stopped dancing, and listened carefully.

"Another bizarre crime has occurred in the town of Thunder Lake, Pennsylvania. As you may know, the community has experienced two mysterious teenage deaths in the last two months. A boy jumped from the roof of the high school in September, then his brother was drowned in the lake on Halloween night. Several witnesses have blamed the deaths on 'monsters,' but police have been skeptical. Believing the crimes to be the result of teenage pranks, the police have stationed guard dogs at Lovers' Lane and the local cemetery, two popular teenage hangouts . . ."

Jessie sighed impatiently. "Come on, get on with it," she groaned. "Tell me something I don't know. *What happened last night?*"

The radio announcer took a breath and continued. "This morning, at approximately six o'clock, the grounds keeper of Thunder Lake Cemetery made a shocking discovery. Killer, the police dog who was guarding the cemetery at night, had been decapitated. His head was impaled on the cemetery gate. And his body was nowhere to be found . . ."

Jessie gasped.

She stared at the blood on her sheets and clenched her stomach in her hands. She felt like she was going to be sick.

"The police were called immediately," the announcer went on. "And when they searched the cemetery, they made another shocking discovery. The graves of the two recently deceased boys had been dug open . . . and their bodies stolen."

The room was spinning now, as Jessie leaned against her dresser, gasping for air. The sunlit room was fading fast, everything turning black.

And the last thing Jessie saw before she fainted and collapsed was her own reflection in the mirror . . .

It was the face of a fourteen-year-old girl.

With the eyes of a monster.

7

Monsters Among Us

From the Thunder Lake High School morning announcements . . .

Attention, all students. This is Principal Frear speaking. I'm sure most of you have heard about last night's incident at Thunder Lake Cemetery. The graves of Moose and Mike Morgan were robbed. And the police seem to think that some of our students are responsible for this atrocious crime.

This kind of behavior is completely unacceptable. Not only is it illegal, it is morally reprehensible. I can't imagine what the Morgan family must be going through now.

As principal of this school, I beg you to come forward and speak if you have any information about the incident. As a human being, I pity the monsters among us who committed this horrible crime . . .

Because heaven may not have such pity on your souls.

Like a stone dropped into a pond, Principal Frear's morning announcement sent rippling waves of shock throughout the school . . .

"Why would someone steal dead bodies?"

"Maybe it's like that music video. You know the one, where that guy dances with a chick's corpse."

"Who did he mean by 'monsters among us?' The cheerleaders?"

"No, your mother."

By lunchtime, everyone was playing the guessing game: Who committed the crime—and why? Most people suspected Jimbo and Crusher, two football players who swore they saw monsters drown Mike Morgan in the lake. Others suspected Heather Leigh Clark, simply because she was head cheerleader and deserved to be locked up. Other theories included spontaneous human combustion, alien abduction, and encounters with angels.

Of course, no one heard Jessie Frank's theory . . .

Because Jessie was slowly losing her mind, pushing through the crowded halls of the school, muttering under her breath—and searching for Sara and Eddie.

She looked at her watch. Twelve-thirty. Which meant they were eating lunch in the cafeteria.

By the time she reached the lunchroom, Jessie was frantic. Her short dark hair was pasted to her forehead with sweat, and her heart was pounding so fast, she thought it would explode. Pushing open the cafeteria doors, she scanned the room, table after table. Finally, in the corner, she saw them . . .

"Sara! Eddie!"

Jessie ran to the small table at the end of the cafeteria and collapsed onto an empty seat.

Sara looked up from her lunch. Her face was as pale as a ghost's. "Jessie!" she gasped. "I've been looking for you all day. Is everything okay? Is Josh still in his cage?"

"We're trying to figure out what happened at the cemetery last night," Eddie explained. "It had to be Josh. He must have escaped."

Jessie sighed and buried her face in her hands.

"It wasn't Josh," she whispered.

Sara glanced at Eddie, then studied her best friend. Jessie's hands were trembling, nervously hiding the tears that were flowing down her face. Sara offered a napkin to Jessie, who blew her nose and sniffled, then stared up at them with red, swollen eyes. Finally, she managed to speak . . .

"I know what happened at the cemetery last night."

Sara dropped her sandwich. "What . . . how . . . ?"

Jessie's eyes glistened with tears. "Because I woke up this morning covered with mud . . . and blood . . ."

Sara and Eddie were too shocked to speak.

Jessie sighed again. There were no tears in her eyes now. Only bitterness. And acceptance. She stared across the cafeteria, watching the other students eating their lunches.

"Nobody knows," she whispered. "All these kids here, who think growing up is hell. They wake up every day and agonize over what to wear and who to date. Nobody knows what hell really is. I can tell you what hell is. Hell is feeling something grow inside of you. Something you can't control. Something monstrous . . ."

She looked at Sara with cold, dead eyes.

Sara shivered. Because Jessie's eyes were as cold and dead as Josh's. They hardly looked human.

"I had dreams last night," said Jessie. "Dreams of running through the woods, hunting a squirrel, killing it . . . and eating it. Then I dreamed I was climbing over the cemetery gates, searching for Mike Morgan's tomb. And the last thing I remember is digging . . . digging into the ground with my hands . . . digging up his grave."

Sara frowned. "Then what?"

"Then I woke up," said Jessie. "My hands and feet were caked with mud and dirt. Blood, too, on my mouth."

Sara looked down at the table and shook her head. "I can't believe it," she whispered. "How could you carry two bodies out of the graveyard? You're not strong enough . . ."

Jessie sighed. "Maybe superhuman strength runs in my family. Maybe I have grave-digging in my blood."

"Or maybe you didn't do it," said Eddie. "Did you check Josh today? Are you sure he's in his cage?"

Jessie shrugged her shoulders. "I forgot to feed him this morning. I was too upset."

"Well, maybe it was him," Eddie went on. "He broke out of that cage once before. He could do it again."

"He's in a coma, Eddie," said Sara.

"Well, maybe so, but I'd feel better if we went to check on him after school."

"I have cheerleading practice after school," said Jessie.

"That's okay. Eddie and I'll do it." Sara took a deep breath and reached for Jessie's hand across the table.

"Jessie, I want you to do me a favor."

"Name it."

"I want you to keep a diary."

"A diary? What for?"

Sara stared deeply into Jessie's eyes. "I want a written document of everything you do, everything you think, everything you feel. Your ups, your downs, your every emotion, no matter how weird or how normal it seems. And I want you start writing now, today, with the date and time for each entry."

Jessie looked down at her hands. "You want to see if the pattern fits Josh's journal, don't you? You want to see how much time I have left . . . before I turn into a monster."

Tears welled up in Sara's eyes. She squeezed Jessie's hand and choked on her words. "I want to help you."

Jessie tried to smile.

"Maybe it's not what you think it is," Sara went on. "Maybe it's just a simple case of sleepwalking. Maybe it's stress. Or maybe it's just, I don't know, puberty or something."

Jessie rolled her eyes. "Oh, please."

Eddie leaned forward. "Don't look now, but we're about to be blessed with the company of Jimbo and Crusher."

Sara and Jessie looked up to see the two hulking football players plodding across the cafeteria, charging right toward them.

"Good afternoon, geek-heads," grunted Jimbo, pulling up a chair. Crusher sat down next to him and cracked his knuckles.

Sara glared at them. "What do you guys want?"

Crusher smirked. "Don't bust a vein, blondie. Just keep talking to your personal *nerd* processor." He nudged Eddie with his elbow.

Jimbo laughed. "Yeah, we're here to talk to little miss Jessie."

Jessie sunk down in her seat. "Me? Why?"

Crusher leaned back in his chair. "We were going to talk to Principal Frear, but then we decided to talk to you first. After all, you saved our butts when you told the cops about those two monsters who killed Mike Morgan."

"I never said they were monsters," Jessie snapped.

"Maybe not," said Crusher. "But the cops were ready to haul me and Jimbo off to jail, and you told them it wasn't us."

Suddenly Jimbo jumped. "But you saw them, didn't you? The monsters?"

Jessie squirmed. "It was too dark. I saw two strangers, that's all."

Jimbo scowled in disbelief, and Crusher continued. "Well, anyway, Jimbo here lives right next door to . . . guess where? That's right, Thunder Lake Cemetery. And guess who he saw in the graveyard last night?"

Jessie closed her eyes, hardly able to speak. "Who?" she whispered.

Jimbo leaned up against her and grinned. "I'm lookin' at her!"

Jessie's eyes popped open. "What happened? What did you see?"

Jimbo and Crusher leaned back and laughed. "You're a wild thing, girl, I'll tell you that!" Jimbo howled. "The way you scaled that gate, hoppin' from gravestone to gravestone! You are one freaky girl!"

Jessie's face started to turn red. Sara and Eddie looked on in horror—half expecting Jessie to explode right before their eyes. Sara couldn't take it any longer . . .

"Look," she said, eyeing up the two boys. "Did you see her do anything illegal? Did you see her dig up the bodies of the Morgan brothers? Did you see her drag them out of the cemetery? Did you? *Did you?*"

Jimbo stared down at the table. "Well . . . uh . . . no."

Crusher rested his huge jaw on his hands. "That's what we were gonna ask you, Jess. How'd you do it? How'd a little girl like you drag them big heavy boys out of the graveyard? Don't see how you coulda done it all by yourself. Unless, of course, you had *helpers.*" He turned and stared at Sara and Eddie.

Sara glared back. "Just what are you insinuating?"

Crusher shrugged. "Oh, I ain't insinuatin' nothin', sweet cheeks. We just figured you nerdy-turdy science geeks were up to some sort of weird experiment or somethin'. And we want to know what's up."

Suddenly Jessie jumped up from the table. Her hair was standing on end, her eyes burning with rage. "Listen, you jockstraps, if we needed bodies for experiments, we'd probably use dumb animals like *you*! So get your fat suspicious heads out of my face or maybe I'll tell the cops a *different* story as to who killed Mike Morgan! Now leave us alone!"

Jimbo and Crusher stared up at Jessie in shock. At first, they couldn't move. Then, scrambling to their feet, they tripped over each other trying to get away.

Jessie took a deep breath and sat down. Sara and Eddie stared in amazement.

"Gee, Jess," said Eddie. "Maybe you should forget cheerleading and join the football team."

Jessie was too shaken to laugh. She slumped down in her chair and pouted like a baby. "He saw me," she whispered. "Jimbo saw me in the cemetery last night. That proves it. That proves I was there."

Sara slapped her hand on the table. "But it doesn't prove that you stole those bodies, Jessie. It doesn't prove anything."

Jessie looked up at Sara and shook her head. "Why are you being so blind, Sara?" she snarled. "I'm cursed, I'm evil, I'm a monster! It's in my blood, Sara, and *you can't change it!* Why won't you face the facts?"

Bursting into tears, Jessie jumped up and ran from the cafeteria.

And Sara whispered to herself . . .

"Because I can't stand the thought of losing you, Jessie."

8

The Love That Never Dies

From the diary of Sara Watkins . . .

The last song Josh ever wrote for me was a love song. In sweet and simple words, he described the eternal power of his feelings, of "the heart that beats forever, the love that never dies."

I, in my foolishness and grief, tried to make his words come true by resurrecting his dead body. But stitches and electrodes are not the way to keep love alive. Love is a universal truth that lives forever in our hearts and souls, not our bodies. It is all-powerful, all-consuming, everlasting . . .

And where there is love, there is pain.

A cold breeze whipped across the lake, lashing the bare trees on the shore with invisible fury. The wind's only weapon was its icy force. Its only master was winter itself. And its only victims were chained to the earth, slaves to the savage passing of the seasons . . .

Like Sara and Eddie.

They pedaled as fast as they could on their bikes along the edge of Thunder Lake, their faces stung by the November cold. Sara tried to blink back her tears, but the wind was too fierce—and her heart too weak.

All she could think about was Josh and Jessie, and how much she loved them.

In the distance, she spotted the highest tower of the Frank family mansion. It rose up in the sky like a giant pointed finger, accusing the heavens of all the misery and suffering that had befallen the House of Frankenstein.

But Sara knew it wasn't heaven's fault.

The curse of Frankenstein was a man-made horror. And she herself had taken part in its making.

The tears on her face began to freeze. She glanced at Eddie and pedaled faster toward the house. He smiled grimly as he pedaled after her.

Soon, they pulled their bikes up to the stone path in front of the mansion. Sara leaned her bike against the porch railing, looked up—and gasped . . .

She was about to be attacked by a growling beast.

But it was only Baskerville, running around the side of the house to greet them, barking loudly and wagging his tail.

"Baskerville!" Sara shouted, reaching down to stroke his black ears. "What are you doing here?"

The dog jumped up and licked her face. Eddie laughed as he set down his bike. "Isn't he supposed to be locked up in the old mill?"

"Yeah," said Sara, kissing Baskerville's nose. "How did you get out, Basker-pooch? Huh? Tell me."

The black hound barked and jumped six feet in the air. "Maybe he busted the door down," said Eddie. "Look at him jump! He seems stronger than ever.

Maybe that thunderstorm a couple nights ago gave him a little shock or something."

Sara frowned. "You know, you could be right," she said, thinking to herself. "You don't suppose . . ." She stopped and scratched her head.

Eddie looked up. "What?"

Sara crouched down and rubbed Baskerville's neck, inspecting the electrodes that pierced the dog's throat. "I just came up with a new theory," she said. "About last night. What if Baskerville broke out of the mill last night, then came home to find Jessie sleepwalking. He followed her to the cemetery and killed the watchdog to protect her. Then, after Jessie started digging up the grave, Baskerville finished the job for her."

Eddie tilted his head and studied the dog at his feet. "Well, he's strong enough to do it. It's hard to believe that Jessie could drag those bodies away. But Frankendog here could do it. Especially if that thunderstorm gave him an extra zap of juice."

Sara stood up and turned toward the house. "If the storm gave Baskerville more strength," she said slowly, "then I wonder if it affected Josh."

Eddie shrugged his shoulders. "Well, we came out here to check on him. Let's go." He reached for the front door and pushed it open.

Sara hesitated. The shadows in the house seemed to be crying out to her—warning her . . .

Eddie stepped inside, then turned around. "Are you coming, Sara?"

Sara took a deep breath. "I'm right behind you."

Together, they entered the dark entrance hall of

the mansion. Everything in the house—the hallway, the clock, the stairs—was shrouded in shadows. And everything brought back painful memories to Sara. Memories of Josh, when he was alive. When he raced her up the stairs. When he played music on his guitar. When he held her and kissed her.

Josh . . .

Sara felt the tears melting on her face as she followed Eddie down the hall to the basement door. He turned the knob and flicked a switch, then descended the old wooden stairs. Sara stood there for a moment, looking down, hesitating, her heart pounding in her chest.

Then she heard something that made her blood run cold . . .

"Sa . . . ra!"

It was Josh's voice, echoing in the basement.

"Sa . . . ra!"

He was awake at last, freed from the prison of his coma. But instead of joy, Sara felt a sickening sense of dread.

"Sa . . . ra!"

That voice. So lonely, so desperate, so filled with pain. It shook the strongest rafters of the house—and touched the darkest corners of Sara's soul.

Sara stood at the top of the stairs, listening. She couldn't move, she couldn't breathe . . .

What's wrong with me? she wondered. Why don't I run down there to embrace the boy I love?

She knew the answer—she was afraid. Afraid to risk her heart again. Afraid to love when love brought nothing but pain.

"Sara? Are you coming down?" Eddie's voice
sounded a million miles away. "Josh is awake now.
He's calling for you, Sara."

"I know," she whispered to herself.

Then slowly, step by step, she descended the stair-
case and walked through the basement room.

Josh was pacing back and forth in his cage. His
hair was tangled across his face, his arms reaching
out through the bars. Reaching for her . . .

"*Sa . . . ra!*"

She stopped in the middle of the room, staring at
the thing in the cage. His body was covered with
bandages and scars, his veins and arteries bulging
against the gray flesh. He looked bigger and fiercer
than she'd ever seen him before. More powerful, more
dangerous.

But the scariest thing about him was his eyes.

They glowed with life—and longing.

"*Sa . . . ra!*"

She couldn't stop staring at those horrible, lonely
eyes. Eyes filled with pain and tears. Like her own.

Slowly he opened his mouth, his parched lips
quivering with torment. He was trying to speak again,
struggling with words that tortured his soul. Finally,
he spoke . . .

"*Love . . . you.*"

Sara burst into tears—and collapsed onto the floor.
Eddie rushed to her side, crouching down and holding her in his arms. The whole basement seemed to
be spinning. Sara pressed her face against Eddie's
chest, trying to block out the sight of that thing, that
monster—the boy she once loved. But even with her

eyes shut, she could feel his presence. And hear his pain . . .

"*Love . . . you . . . Sa . . . ra.*"

Sara threw herself down on the floor, sobbing out of control. She cursed the name of Frankenstein. She cursed the day she brought Josh back to life. But most of all, she cursed the love in her own heart.

"Why?" she gasped, pounding the basement floor with her fist. "Why?"

Eddie squeezed her shoulders. "It's okay, Sara. I'm here. Don't be afraid," he whispered.

Sara looked up through her tears at the thing in the cage. He was so monstrous, so sad, so miserable—and it was all her fault. "Why?" she gasped again. "Why do people fall in love?"

Eddie stroked her long blond hair and whispered, "Shhh." But Sara couldn't stop. Her heart was about to burst, and she had to speak her mind, get it all out . . .

"My love destroyed him," she said. "And now his love is destroying me. It's so . . . cruel . . . so unfair. Everything I love is taken away from me . . . even Jessie . . . and love makes it hurt all the more."

Eddie pressed himself closer. "Shhh." He whispered in her ear and kissed her neck.

Sara's head snapped around. "Don't, Eddie!" she cried. "Don't love me. Can't you see? I'm like Josh and Jessie. I'm cursed." She covered her face with her hands and muttered under her breath, "Love me and die."

Eddie pulled away slowly. He looked down at Sara, then up at the bandaged creature in the cage. "I'm not afraid of death, Sara," he whispered. "And I'm not afraid of getting hurt, either. Nothing hurts more than living without love. And living without love is like death, but worse. We're only human, Sara. We can't help falling in love."

Sara closed her eyes and pictured Josh and Jessie, the way they used to be.

Eddie was right. She couldn't imagine living without them.

Slowly, she raised her head, pushing the hair from her eyes, and looked up at Eddie. "I don't want to fall in love with you, Eddie," she said. "Because I'm afraid."

Eddie nodded. His long black hair framed his face, his dark eyes gleaming with love and concern. He reached out with his hand and helped Sara to her feet. "Come on," he said. "We did what we came here to do. Josh is fine. He hasn't escaped his cage. So let's try to find a way to help Jessie."

He pulled Sara toward the stairs, but she wouldn't move. "Wait," she said. Then, turning toward the cage, she approached Josh slowly.

The creature looked out through the bars, his face twisted by scars, his eyes burning with passion. He opened his mouth but didn't speak. Instead he reached out with a huge trembling hand—a hand that was not really his own—and touched Sara's face . . .

"Josh," she whispered.

The creature tried to smile.

"*Sa . . . ra.*"

And for one brief moment, everything seemed possible again—hopes and dreams and love everlasting.

Reflected in the eyes of a teenage girl and a resurrected monster was something that transcended time itself. Their souls were bound forever by the one thing that makes us all human . . .

Love and love alone.

A tear trickled down Sara's face. Josh gently wiped it away with his finger. They stood there in silence, painfully aware of the bars between them—and the cruel hands of fate that tore them apart.

But still, in spite of it all, they loved . . .

And that was all that mattered.

Sara reached down and pulled the Frank family ring off her finger. She held it up in front of Josh, watching the glint of recognition flash in his cold, dead eyes. Then she held his massive hand and carefully placed the gold ring in his palm. The creature's hand closed over the ring. And Sara turned away.

Eddie was waiting for her at the foot of the stairs. His dark eyes were filled with tears. His heart, too, was breaking.

Sara crossed the basement room slowly, her whole body trembling. In her soul, she knew she would love Josh forever. But in her mind, she knew it was time to pick up the pieces of her life. To help Jessie. To comfort Eddie. And to save herself.

And yet, as she climbed the stairs one by one, passing from darkness into light, she heard the words echo once more in the basement—words that would haunt her for all eternity . . .

"Love . . . you . . . Sa . . . ra."

9

The Diary of Jessie Frank

From a note to Sara Watkins from Jessie Frank . . .

Dear Sara: Here's the diary you asked me to keep—in all its gruesome glory.

I have to admit, I'm a little ashamed to let you read it. Only two days have passed since I started writing, and already it sounds like the ramblings of a serial killer. It's hard to believe I wrote it. Am I really that crazy? Am I really that dangerous? And the question that scares me most of all . . .

Will I destroy everyone around me?

Like it or not, here it is—the diary of yours truly,

Jessie Frank

November 12th, 1:35 P.M.

I'm sitting here in science class. Bored out of my mind. Miss Nevils is rambling. I think I hate her.

The sun is shining through the windows. The light is hitting the posters on the wall—you know, all those pictures of the digestive system, the circulatory system, the nervous system. I'm thinking what pretty colors they are. They're such beautiful posters, I can't believe I never really looked at them before.

Then I look up at Miss Nevils. She's talking on and on about photosynthesis. I can't help staring at her and wondering . . .

What would Miss Nevils look like if I ripped her body open? Would she be as pretty as the posters on the wall?

2:15 P.M.

I'm in study hall now. A couple weird things happened on the way here.

First, I was walking down the hall, holding my books over my chest, as usual. Then I started noticing the boys. Not just the cute ones. All of them. Suddenly I wanted them to look at me. So I lowered my books and stuck out my chest. I swayed my hips as I walked. I smiled at every boy I passed. I even winked at a few!

I could feel myself burning up inside. It was like a fire in my body, raging out of control.

I ran to the girls' room, not to cool down but to fix my makeup. I hardly wear any at all, but today I wanted to look gorgeous, irresistible. So I pushed open the bathroom door and marched up to the sink with my purse.

Who should be there but every tough girl in the school. You know who I mean—Kathy and Johanna and Melinda, with their leather jackets and teased hair. And they're puffing away on cigarettes and blowing the smoke in my face.

So I turned to them and said, "Do you mind?"

Well, they got all bent out of shape and started hassling me. "Look here, you little twerp," said Melinda, the ringleader. "You got a lot of nerve, being a freshman and all. This is *our* smoking lounge. So, *scram.*"

I don't know what came over me.

First, I slammed Melinda against the wall. "Don't bug me, you ugly tramp," I snarled. "Or I'll stick that cigarette so far up your nose, you'll have the surgeon general's warning burned in your brain. If you have a brain."

The next thing I knew the other two girls, Kathy and Johanna, grabbed me and held me in a headlock. Then they dragged me across the floor toward the stalls. Melinda shouted out something about a "toilet shampoo," and I figured they were going to dunk my head and flush.

I barely remember what happened next. I think my animal instincts took over. First, I saw red. Then, I exploded.

Screaming at the top of my lungs, I broke away from them and spun around. Normally, I'd run away. But not this time. This time, I attacked. With my fists, my fingernails, my teeth . . .

In other words, I went nuts. Absolutely nuts.

By the time I came to my senses, Kathy and Johanna were lying in a heap under the sink, drenched in water. And Melinda was knocked unconscious, her head hanging down in a toilet that kept flushing and flushing.

I couldn't believe what I had done. I'd beaten the crap out of the three toughest girls in the school!

But I didn't feel victorious. I felt afraid. Very afraid.

2:34 P.M.

I'm still stuck in study hall.

I don't know why, but I feel like singing. Out loud. So I do. I sing as loud as I can. And then I get yelled at.

Still, I can't stop. I tilt back my head, open my mouth, and belt out another chorus of "Girls Just Wanna Have Fun." Everybody's looking at me, but I don't care.

Then the teacher sends me to the principal's office. I jump out of my seat and dance my way out the door and down the hall.

I'm not going to the principal's office.

I'm climbing the stairs to the top of the school. Now I'm dancing on the rooftop. Dancing and singing for all of Thunder Lake. I dance near the edge of the roof, and I look down at the sidewalk—where Moose Morgan fell to his death.

And I laugh and laugh and laugh.

How could he die from such a fall? The concrete looks so soft, so inviting . . .

If I jumped, I wouldn't get hurt.

I'd fly.

3:45 P.M.

I'm in the girls' locker room. School's over, and it's time for cheerleading practice. I changed into my uniform real fast so I wouldn't have to hang out with the other girls.

I'm afraid I'll do something crazy.

So I'm sitting in the corner with my notebook, as far away from the lockers as I can get. I can hear the voices of the other cheerleaders. They're all so perky and happy, I hate them.

But no, stop it, Jessie. Don't blow it.

I've got to stay calm. I can't let my emotions control me.

There's Heather Leigh Clark, running around like a mother hen. "Come on, girls," she says. "I want to see you all on the gym floor in exactly sixty seconds. Move it!" Then she blows this stupid little whistle, and I want to jam the thing down her throat.

Where are these feelings coming from? Why can't I control them?

Well, I have to go now. It's time to jump around on the gym floor and scream, "Go, team, go!"

I hope I don't kill anybody.

5:42 P.M.

Cheerleading practice is over.

The same can probably be said about my career as a cheerleader.

Here's what happened.

Cindi Boyer, captain of the freshman cheerleaders, was leading us through our cheers. You know, "Push 'em back, push 'em back, waaaay back!" It's a simple basic cheer with foot-stomping and hand-clapping.

Simple, yeah, but I screwed it up anyway.

And who should see me but Heather Leigh Clark. She came storming across the gym, blowing her stupid whistle. "You! Jessie Frank! You're doing it wrong! Wrong, wrong, *wrong*!" She started throwing a hissy fit, and made me step out of line. "It's stomp, clap, clap, stomp, clap, clap!" She demonstrated the cheer, then turned those snake eyes on me. "Now you do it, Frank. And do it *right*!"

I stood in front of the other cheerleaders, feeling like a fool. I could feel the blood boiling inside of me. I wanted to scream.

But I didn't.

Instead, I did six cartwheels and three handsprings across the gym floor!

Which amazed everyone. Especially me. I stink at gymnastics. I've never done a handspring in my life!

Some of the cheerleaders started clapping—and that made Heather Leigh Clark furious.

"Listen, Frank!" she hissed through her teeth. "We work as a *team*, or not at all. There's no room for *show-offs*! So get back in line and do it *right*! Come on, now, everybody! Let's go! *Push 'em back, push 'em back, waaaay back*! Get in step, Frank! *Push 'em back, push 'em back*, lift your head, Frank!"

For the next thirty minutes, she watched me like a hawk—yelling, screaming, accusing me of everything but murder.

And believe me, murder was on my mind.

I could feel my face turning red, the hot blood surging through my veins. I clenched my hands and gritted my teeth until my whole body was wracked with pain.

Then I looked down at my hands . . .

They were covered with blood.

I couldn't believe my eyes. I had dug my own fingernails so deep into my palms, I'd broken the skin! Blood was flowing from my hands, drop by drop, onto the gym floor.

One of the freshman cheerleaders screamed.

Then everyone was staring at me in horror. Except Heather. I swear that girl had a smirk on her face!

"Something wrong, Frank?" she sneered.

I glared and gritted my teeth so hard, my jaws ached.

"Don't just stand there, Frank," Heather went on. "Go to the locker room and clean yourself up. Now! Move it! And bring back some paper towels to clean up the mess you made!"

The whole gym was silent. Everyone watched me cross the floor toward the locker room. It was the longest walk of my life. I'd never felt so humiliated.

All I could think was, "I hate you, Heather Leigh Clark. I hate you with all my soul. And I'll get you for this."

In the locker room, I walked to the sink and put my hands under running water. Then I looked at myself in the mirror . . .

There was blood on my lips, my teeth, my gums.

I'd bitten myself!

At first, I felt like screaming. Then, something weird came over me. I felt like smiling. Grinning with a big mouth full of blood. Looking at myself in the mirror and laughing.

And that's when I started crying. Uncontrollably.

It took me a few minutes to calm down. I splashed water on my hands, face, and mouth—trying to wash away every last drop of this awful curse that's driving me crazy.

But I know it's impossible. I'm doomed.

Finally, I took some paper towels out to the gym to clean up the blood. The cheerleaders continued to practice as I bent down to wipe the red stains off the floor. I could feel everyone looking at me.

And I hated every single one of them.

"Get back in line, Frank!" Heather Leigh Clark snapped. "The Homecoming game is less than a week away! You're wasting everyone's time!"

I jumped up and stuffed the bloody paper towels in my shirt and started cheering . . .

"Kill 'em all! Kill 'em all! Allll dead!!"

8:30 P.M.

I'm home now, in my bedroom, on my bed.

I was surprised to see Baskerville here. He must have broken out of the old mill. He was sitting on the front porch, waiting for me to come home. Like the old days.

I waved to him and shouted out his name, and he came running down the stone path to greet me.

But then he stopped.

He stood about five feet in front of me, staring at me and sniffing the air. I said, "Baskerville, it's me, baby!"

And he growled at me.

I reached out to pet him, but he snarled and snapped at my fingers. Then he turned and ran around the side of the house.

My own dog hates me.

I don't blame him. I hate myself, too. And so what? Who cares?

I was hungry, and that's all that mattered to me. So I came into the house and went straight to the kitchen. I opened the fridge and ransacked every shelf, but I couldn't find anything appetizing. Gosh, I was hungry! I was starving to death!

That's when I remembered the bloody paper towel stuffed in my shirt. I was so upset about cheerleading practice, I didn't change my clothes. The towel was still pressed against my chest.

I reached in and pulled it out, holding it up to admire the dark red stain. The stain was shaped like an animal, maybe a dog. It was beautiful.

The next thing I knew, I stuffed the paper towel in my mouth and chewed it up and swallowed it.

Then I started to cry.

I'm feeling much better now. My mind is clear. My wounds are healing. Everything is going to be okay.

But there's something I should tell you.

I never changed the dirty, bloody sheets on my bed.

I'm lying on them now.

It feels good.

November 13th, 9:15 A.M.

Here I am, back at school. Another day. History class. Oh, joy.

I'm bored out of my skull, but that's normal. I hate history. Who cares about a bunch of dead people? I'm so bored I could scream.

But I won't. I'll listen to the teacher like a good little girl.

He's talking about the Vikings. Killing. Pillaging. Burning down villages.

And now I'm laughing.

Out loud.

Laughing, laughing, laughing.

Death can be so funny. Ha ha.

12:28 P.M.

I can't eat my lunch. I'm too upset.

I'm hiding beneath the bleachers in the gym, crying my eyes out, and wondering if there's any hope for me.

I don't want to be a monster.

I want everything to be the way it used to be. I want my friends. I want my family. I want my dog. I want to fall in love and live happily ever after.

I want to be human again.

Is that too much to ask for?

3:28 P.M.

Almost time for cheerleading practice.

I've got to be strong. I've got to fight this thing inside of me, this monster, this curse. I've got to destroy the evil that flows through my blood . . .

Or die trying.

5:05 P.M.

I don't know where to begin.

Cheerleading practice is over. I'm sitting in an empty classroom, writing it all down before I forget. My head is spinning. It's hard to concentrate. Everything's a blur.

I remember changing into my uniform in the locker room and going out to the gym for practice. Some of the cheerleaders want to know if I feel okay—and if my hands still hurt from yesterday. I show them the scars. They say "yuck" and turn away.

Then I get in line and start cheering. I'm doing good, real good. I'm clapping when I'm supposed to clap and stomping when I'm supposed to stomp. I'm feeling great. About myself. About everything.

Now here's the part that gets all jumbled up in my head . . .

I remember Heather Leigh Clark standing in front of me. She's saying something, I don't know what. But she's unhappy. She's yelling. She's shaking her fist.

I want to hit her but I don't.

I resist the urge.

I fight the monster within.

And then everything goes black.

It turns out that I fainted on the floor of the gym! When I opened my eyes, the whole cheerleading squad was crouched down around me, asking, "Are you okay, Jessie? Are you all right?"

And get this . . .

Heather Leigh Clark had tears in her eyes!

Her face was white, and her hand was stroking my forehead. "I'm sorry, Jessie," she said. "I'm really, *really* sorry. I pushed you too hard, I know."

I was in shock. I couldn't speak.

Why was Heather being so nice to me?

"You know how sorry I am," she said. "You're not going to tell anyone, are you?"

Then I figured it out. She was afraid of getting in trouble! It wouldn't look good if the head cheerleader made a poor sick girl faint.

"Don't worry, Heather," I said. "I'm fine."

I tried to get up, but she stopped me. "Just lie there a minute and relax," she said. "You can go home as soon as you feel better. And don't worry about practice. You're doing great, Jessie. You'll make a *terrific* cheerleader."

"Gee, thanks, Heather," I said.

After a minute or two I got up, went to the locker room, and changed my clothes. I felt happy, and relieved. I couldn't stop smiling . . .

Because I won.

I faced the monster inside of me—and beat it! I looked it in the eye, saw the hate and fury burning there, and pushed it away through the sheer force of my will.

So maybe there's hope after all.

Maybe I *can* have friends and family and love everlasting. In spite of the curse. In spite of the horror. In spite of the voice that cries out in my head . . .

"Kill Heather Leigh Clark. Kill her tonight."

The Girl Most Likely (to Die)

From a song by Josh Frank, written one year before
his suicide . . .

> I see her walking down the hall.
> I see her shopping at the mall.
> I see her dressed up like a doll.
> She's the girl most likely.
>
> You know she's always rich and thin.
> You know she always plays to win.
> You know she always hides her sin.
> She's the girl most likely.
>
> She's the girl most likely to make it.
> She's the girl most likely to fake it.
> She's the girl most likely to lie.
> She's the girl most likely (to die).

The Thunder Valley Shopping Mall stretched out
like a sleeping giant on a bed of dark rolling mountains. The sun had long vanished from the sky, but the
storefronts of the mall blazed with unearthly light, a
strange peach-colored glow that illuminated the far-

thest reaches of the parking lot.

Heather Leigh Clark cursed under her breath.

Stupid shoppers. I wish they'd all die.

The mall was so crowded tonight she couldn't find a spot to park her beloved BMW. Even the *Handicapped Only* spaces were taken.

Good-for-nothing *cripples*, she thought. Why don't they just *kill* them all at *birth*?

She steered and turned down another row of parked cars, cursing at the darkened headlights. They seemed to be laughing at her—a thousand pairs of eyes, laughing, mocking, and tormenting her. She shook her head and drove on. After ten minutes of searching, she was forced to face the horrible truth . . .

She was going to have to park on the farthest edge of the lot—and walk half a mile to the mall.

I should just take my money *elsewhere*, she thought. To *hell* with this stupid mall.

But she knew there was nowhere else to go at this time of night—nowhere else she could buy a new dress for Homecoming.

So she parked her BMW in the last space on the edge of the lot and turned off the ignition. She grabbed her purse (full of daddy's charge cards), got out of the car and locked the door. Then taking a deep breath, Heather Leigh Clark started the long trek toward the shining lights of the mall.

Her shoes clicked on the concrete, the eerie sound echoing across the lot. She glanced nervously at the shadows between the parked cars and tightened her grip on her purse. It was was a little too dark and a little too scary.

A girl could get killed out here, she thought. And no one would ever know.

Eddie looked at himself in the department store mirror and shook his head. "I can't believe I'm doing this."

Sara reached up to adjust his tie. "Stop complaining," she said. "you look gorgeous in a suit."

And he did. The rich black fabric of the suit brought out the dark gleam in his eyes and the luster in his black flowing hair. Sara thought he looked like a movie star.

"It's a very handsome suit," said the saleslady. "Will this be cash or charge?"

Eddie sighed. "Cash," he said. Then he turned to Sara and whispered, "A *waste* of cash."

Sara rolled her eyes. "What do you care, Eddie? Your mom's paying for it. She's thrilled about this, isn't she? And who else could be my escort for Homecoming? Josh? I don't think so."

Eddie shrugged. "Okay," he said. "I'll buy it and I'll wear it. For you, Sara."

Sara smiled. "Thanks, Eddie."

Then Eddie stepped back into the dressing room and pulled the curtain shut. The saleslady walked away to ring up the purchase. And Sara whispered through the curtain, "Now you have to help me pick out a dress."

Eddie groaned.

But deep down, he was thrilled. He had never hung out at the mall with friends before. It was kind of fun.

And who knows? Maybe Sara would be crowned Homecoming Queen. Their pictures would appear in the town paper and the school yearbook. For one magical night, they'd be Thunder Lake's most celebrated couple.

And stuck-up Heather Leigh Clark would be eating her heart out.

The blond cheerleader marched through the mall with her nose in the air. Clutching her purse and walking briskly, she waved at a group of classmates leaning against a fountain—but she didn't stop and talk to them. She didn't have the time.

Heather Leigh Clark was on a mission.

She needed a dress—and not just any dress. It had to be the most beautiful dress in the mall, the most ravishing fashion money could buy. Daddy would pay for it, of course. Anything for his precious little girl.

Jimbo and Crusher were standing by the entrance of the department store, wearing football jackets and drinking slurpies. Heather tried to sneak past them. She didn't have time to flirt—even with the new captain of the football team.

"Hey, Heather!" Crusher shouted. "Wanna grab some pizza with us?"

Heather sighed. "Sorry, boys," she said. "I have to buy a dress for Homecoming. I'm nominated for Homecoming Queen, you know."

"Cool," said Jimbo.

"Too bad I can't be your escort," said Crusher, slipping a brawny arm around Heather's shoulder. "But I'll be too busy leading our team to victory. It's a tough job, but someone's gotta do it."

"I'm so *sure*," said Heather, slipping away from him. "Excuse me, but I have to buy this dress *tonight*. And the mall's going to close in twenty minutes. *Bye-bye!*"

Then she disappeared in a flash, storming through the store, flying down the aisles—and descending upon the lady's department like a one-woman swarm of locusts.

"Ugly, ugly, *ugly*," she muttered as she searched the racks for the Perfect Dress.

Finally, she found it.

It was stunning. A pale blue silk dress with a plunging neckline. Gorgeous. *Perfect.*

So she grabbed her size and ran to the dressing room to try it on. She stepped into a cubicle, pulled the curtain, and began to unbutton her blouse.

And that's when she heard the voices of Sara Watkins and Eddie Perez.

"You don't think it's too revealing?" said Sara.

"I think it's the most beautiful dress I've ever seen," said Eddie.

They were shopping for Sara's Homecoming dress! Heather couldn't believe her luck. It was the perfect opportunity for her to spy on the competition!

So, pulling back the curtain, Heather peered out at the dressing room mirror . . .

And screamed.

"What do you think you're *doing*, Sara?" she snapped. "You are *not* going to wear that dress!"

Sara and Eddie looked up in shock. They glanced at the pale blue dress hanging from a hook in Heather's cubicle—then looked down at the pale blue dress clinging to Sara's body.

It was the exact same dress.

"*That's* the dress *I* want to wear," Heather hissed. "So take it off right now and start looking for *another* one!"

Sara and Eddie looked at each other and shook their heads. Then Sara turned back to Heather. "Look, Heather," she said. "Eddie and I have been shopping all night."

Heather glanced at the box Eddie was holding. It was from the men's department. "*He's* your escort?" Heather scoffed. "What ever happened to your *boyfriend*, Josh?"

Sara gritted her teeth. "You know Josh is sick, Heather," she muttered. "In fact, I'm helping him with his recovery. I *wish* you'd stop bugging me about Eddie. He's just a friend."

Heather smirked when she saw the disappointment on Eddie's face. "Whatever you say, Sara. Your *friend* can escort you to the Homecoming Game. But you're *not* going to wear *my* dress!"

Sara crossed her arms over her chest and took a deep breath. "Look, Heather." She scowled. "I'm going to wear whatever I want. I'm buying this dress. You can go look for something else or wear the same dress, *I don't care*. It's up to you."

Then Sara spun around, stormed into a cubicle, and closed the curtain. Eddie looked at Heather and shrugged. Heather growled like a dog. Then she grabbed her dress on the hanger and marched out to the sales floor . . .

In search of a More Perfect Dress.

By the time she found something she liked—and paid for it with Daddy's charge card—the mall was almost empty. The stores had switched their lights to half-power, and the shopping center became a gray, lifeless space filled with long, dreary shadows.

Oh, *great*, Heather thought. Now I have to walk half a mile through this *mausoleum* to get back to my car.

A tall security guard stood at the store's entrance to the mall, locking out the last customers of the night. Heather glared at him as she walked by with her purchase. The bag rustled against her hip as she stepped into the huge, gloomy hallway of the mall.

There was nobody in sight. The Muzak had stopped playing and the fountain had ceased bubbling. It seemed as if Heather Leigh Clark was the only living soul left in the mall. She felt like there'd been a nuclear war—and she was the last survivor.

Quickly, nervously, she rushed past the dimmed storefronts. The Yarn Barn. The Jean Machine. Music Explosion. The Kid Vid Arcade. They all looked so dark, so desolate. Like tombs.

Suddenly Heather froze.

She heard something behind her. Footsteps.

Snapping her head around, she looked down the darkened corridor of the mall. Was someone following her? No. Nobody in sight. Just shadows. She turned around and started walking faster.

Chill *out*, Heather, she told herself. You're the only one here.

But as she walked on—past Toyland and the Book Nook—she thought she heard it again. More footsteps. And when she glanced over her shoulder, she swore she saw a black shadow dart behind a plastic shrub.

She turned and looked. The shadow was still there, behind the greenery. Watching. Waiting.

You're *crazy*, Heather, she told herself. You're scared and you're imagining things.

But that didn't make her feel any safer. She clutched her bag and started to walk faster and faster through the mall, glancing over her shoulder as her heels clicked on the gray tile floor and echoed off the walls.

But wait, no. That *wasn't* an echo.

It *was* someone else's footsteps.

As quick as she could, Heather spun around to confront the person following her. And this time, she saw the shadow clearly, ducking behind the slurpie stand . . .

It was definitely human.

And it was definitely stalking her.

Heather's scream pierced the stillness of the mall. Her heart pounding, she turned and started running. Running as fast as she could. Running for her life.

She saw the mall exit in the distance, growing larger and larger. And she heard the footsteps behind her, coming closer and closer. She gasped for breath and cried out as she hurled herself against an exit door.

It was locked.

She spun around madly, pushing against each door—until she found one that was unlocked. Then she stumbled out onto the sidewalk and started racing across the empty parking lot. It was as cold and desolate as a desert at midnight. All the cars were gone now—except Heather's BMW, which sat at the very end of this sprawling stretch of concrete.

"Somebody *help* me!!" she screamed at the air. But no one could hear her—and no one could help her. She was too terrified to look behind her, too frightened of the shadow that pursued her across the dark and empty lot.

Her car was getting closer now. Heather fumbled for her keys as she ran, her heart pounding like a savage tribal drum. Her car was only twenty feet away, ten feet, five feet . . .

Yes, *yes*! she thought as she plunged the key into the lock and swung open the car door.

Then, in less than a second, she was sitting in the driver's seat—slamming and locking the door behind her.

"I *did* it!" she screamed. "I'm safe!"

Catching her breath, she looked out the window at the parking lot behind her.

There was no one there. No shadow. No follower. No crazy psycho trying to kill her.

Heather breathed out a heavy sigh of relief. She didn't know what had happened to her pursuer. But she didn't care. She was safe now. That's all that mattered.

She tilted the rearview mirror to study her face. Her makeup was streaked with tears. She looked awful. So she started wiping the dark lines under her eyes.

And that's when she heard something move in the backseat of the car . . .

And saw the shadow in the rearview mirror . . .

And felt the hands around her throat.

11

Missing Pieces

From *The Coal County Daily News* . . .

> ### THUNDER LAKE TEEN DISAPPEARS
> *Another Unsolved Mystery in Crime-Ridden Town*

From *The Weekly Thunder* . . .

> ### WHAT EVER HAPPENED TO
> ### HEATHER LEIGH CLARK?
> *Head Cheerleader Shops Till She Drops—Out of Sight*

From *The Pennsylvania Scandal* . . .

> ### ATTACK OF THE MALL MARTIANS
> *Aliens Use Charge Cards to Buy Teenage Girls*

Taking a deep breath, Sara Watkins turned the key, opened the door—and stepped into the cage with the monster.

"It's okay, Josh," she whispered. "It's only me. Sara."

The creature looked up at her with dead green eyes. His long black hair fell over his face, hiding the stitches that scarred his flesh. In his massive hand, he held the Frank family ring. The ring he had given Sara on the night he killed himself. The ring she had returned in tears.

"Be careful, Sara," said Eddie, standing by the door of the cage with a hypodermic tranquilizer.

"Everything's okay," said Sara. "Isn't it, Josh? You're feeling better now, aren't you?"

The creature growled but didn't move.

"I've come to remove your bandages," she said softly. "Your wounds are all healed. Now you can put on some clothes. Would you like that, Josh?"

A tiny whimper escaped the creature's lips as Sara knelt down and removed the bandages from his arms and legs. He stared at her face while she worked, never taking his eyes off her.

"I brought you a pair of pants, and a sweatshirt, and a jacket," she said in a calm, soothing voice. "Won't it feel good to be dressed up again?"

The creature nodded his huge head and sighed. His eyes were wet and glistening.

"He seems very peaceful," commented Eddie. "I guess he couldn't have committed those crimes."

Sara lifted Josh's giant legs one by one, slipping the trousers up over his hips. "No, not Josh," she said, gazing into the creature's eyes. "You've been good, haven't you, Josh? You've been resting and growing strong."

Eddie shrugged. "Strong enough to break out of the cage," he said. "But he hasn't. He's been so quiet. Even kind of sad. I wonder why."

Sara lifted Josh's arms and pulled the sweatshirt

over his head and shoulders. She glanced at Eddie. "I think reality has finally sunk in," she whispered. "I think he's finally accepted what he is . . . or what he's become."

Eddie studied the sad expression on the monster's face as Sara helped him into the oversized jacket. He looked like a giant frightened child—abandoned, lonely, and lost. The sight of him made Eddie want to cry. And the loving way Sara treated him touched Eddie's heart.

Eddie cleared his throat. "But, Sara. If Josh didn't rob those graves or attack Heather Leigh Clark, then who did?"

Sara stroked Josh's long hair, then stood up and walked to the door of the cage. Locking it behind her, she turned to face Eddie. "I think it was Jessie," she said flatly.

"Jessie? You really think Jessie did those things?" Eddie couldn't believe Sara would say such a thing. "What made you change your mind?"

Sara leaned against the basement wall and closed her eyes. "Jessie's diary," she said. "I have to admit, it terrified me. She's losing her mind, Eddie. She's turning into a monster. I can't deny the truth any longer."

Eddie shook his head in disbelief. "But . . . but, Sara. Jessie is so sweet. She couldn't . . . kill somebody."

Sara opened her eyes and stared at the tall, dark-haired boy. "Her last words in the diary were, 'Kill Heather Leigh Clark. Kill her tonight.' "

Eddie turned and started pacing the floor of the basement. "Something's wrong," he muttered to himself. "Something's missing. Something we're forgetting."

Sara didn't have a chance to respond. She was interrupted by the sound of a banging door and footsteps on the basement stairs. "It's Jessie," she whispered to Eddie. "She didn't go to school today. I don't know if she's heard the news about Heather."

Eddie nodded—and turned to greet Jessie as she walked through the door of the second basement room. "Hi, Jessie."

"Hi, guys! What's up?"

Eddie and Sara couldn't believe their eyes . . .

Jessie was smiling.

In fact, their short, dark-haired friend was positively radiant. Her round cheeks were pink and glowing. Her eyes sparkled like jewels.

And yes, she was grinning from ear to ear!

"Jessie?" said Sara, in shock. "Are you okay?"

The baby-faced freshman smirked and shrugged. "I'm better than okay, girl," she said. "I'm the best there is. And don't you forget it."

Sara glanced at Eddie, then looked back at Jessie with confusion in her eyes.

"Didn't you read my last diary entry?" said Jessie.

"Ah . . . yeah . . ."

"Well, then you know," Jessie explained. "I can beat this thing. I can fight the monster inside of me. With my mind. With my soul. I know I can do it, Sara."

Sara felt a knot in her stomach.

How could she tell Jessie that Heather Leigh Clark

was missing? And possibly dead.

Jessie took a step closer to Sara and the cage. Josh looked up at his little sister—and snarled.

"What's his problem?" Jessie asked, staring at the thing that used to be Josh.

The creature snarled again and crouched down in the farthest corner of his cage.

"Maybe we should go into the other room," Sara suggested. Jessie gave her a funny look, then shrugged and walked back to the front basement. Eddie and Sara followed.

"Okay, what's up?" said Jessie, leaning against a counter.

Sara bit her lip. She didn't know what to say. Except the facts. "You didn't go to school today, so you haven't heard the news." She took a deep breath. "Heather Leigh Clark is missing."

The smile disappeared from Jessie's face.

"They found her car in the parking lot of the Thunder Valley Mall this morning," Sara explained. "There was blood on the seat. Nothing was stolen. Her charge cards and her Homecoming dress were left in the car. But Heather's gone."

Jessie stared down at the floor. Her lip started to tremble. And tears pooled up in her eyes.

"No," she whispered. "No . . . no . . . no, NO, *NO!*"

Jessie slammed her fists against the counter and dropped to the floor, hugging her legs and crying. She rocked back and forth. She hid her face with her hands. She pulled at her hair.

"It couldn't be me," she sobbed. "I stayed home last night. I felt the monster inside of me, but I fought it!

Honestly, Sara! I beat it! I swear, I didn't lay a hand on Heather Leigh Clark!"

Sara didn't say anything. But she walked over to Jessie, crouched down, and hugged her.

"You believe me, don't you, Sara?" she whispered.

Sara bit her tongue.

But Eddie responded in a soft, gentle voice. "I believe you, Jessie."

The two girls looked up at him, their eyes shining with curiosity—and hope.

Eddie shoved his hands into his pockets and shrugged. "It doesn't make any sense," he said. "All these missing pieces. The dead bodies of the Morgan brothers. The headless carcass of a guard dog. It's almost as if someone is gathering body parts . . . like we did . . . when we resurrected Josh."

Slowly, Sara stood up. "But who?" she asked. "Who else knows the secret of Frankenstein's journal? Only Grandfather Frank, and he's dead."

Eddie rubbed his head. "Maybe he's not."

"What do you mean? Of course he's dead," said Sara. "You helped me drag his body into the freezer. It's right there, behind that door!" She pointed to the huge steel door behind her.

Eddie shrugged. "There's an easy way to find out."

Jessie jumped up. "No! I don't want to gawk at a frozen stiff!"

"Well, then close your eyes," said Eddie, crossing the room toward the freezer door. "I *have* to make sure he's still here."

Jessie covered her eyes with her hands. Sara walked up behind Eddie and took a deep breath. Then, grasping the heavy chrome handle, Eddie swung the door open.

A cloud of icy mist swirled in the air, blinding their vision. Eddie snapped on the light inside the freezer. Slowly, the fog lifted.

And Sara screamed.

"He's gone!"

Jessie ran to the door of the freezer and stopped. She stared down at the bloody sheet on the floor and the shards of broken ice. And her brain reeled in confusion, terror, and shock.

"Grandfather Frank is gone," she muttered.

Eddie stepped into the freezer. "And that's not all that's missing," he said. "Look!" He pointed at the shattered block of ice on the shelf . . .

The block of ice that had contained the frozen head of the original Frankenstein monster.

Sara leaned forward and examined the ice chips. She picked up a bloody shard and turned it in her hands. "Look here," she said. "Teeth marks."

Jessie squinted her eyes. "What does that mean?" she asked. "Did the monster head chew its way out of the ice?"

She meant it as a joke. But no one was laughing.

Eddie pointed at the steel door of the freezer. "Look at this!"

It was a bloody handprint. But not an ordinary handprint. The fingers were twisted and gnarled. Like the hands of Grandfather Frank.

Suddenly Sara began to tremble and cry. "No, it can't be," she whispered. "It can't be true!" Her friends stared at her. "Don't you see? Don't you understand what this means?"

Eddie and Jessie were too shocked to speak.

"I'll tell you what it means," said Sara, on the edge of hysteria. "It's Grandfather Frank, and it's the worst thing that could happen!"

A cold silence fell over the house.

"He's alive," said Sara. "He's alive!"

Her voice cracked.

"And he's making more monsters."

12

Skin Crawler

From the diary of Sara Watkins . . .

What is Good without Evil? What is Light without Darkness? What is Hope without Fear?

These things must exist side by side—or else they have no meaning. Like enemies at war, they struggle within us all.

The discovery of Grandfather Frank's resurrection was both a blessing and a curse. It brought new hope to Jessie, who thought she had committed horrible crimes. But it also struck fear in our hearts, knowing the terrible power he could unleash upon the world.

We had no choice but to take the Bad with the Good . . .

And pray we were on the winning team.

A human cell is an organism with a life of its own. It lives, it feeds, it grows, it reproduces, and it dies.

Hundreds of thousands of these cells interact in a society of sorts—a vast network of forms and functions that, together, create a single life form greater than the sum of its parts.

And this particular life form was called Jessie Frank.

While Jessie experienced the pleasures and pains of human life, the cells of her body faced a different kind of reality. In her flesh and blood, her brain and bones, her muscles and nerves, each and every cell was fighting a long and devastating war against a ruthless enemy—an army of infectious organisms that grew more powerful every day . . .

The curse of Frankenstein.

Long dormant in Jessie's blood, these tiny microbes were sparked to life on the night of the lightning storm. Now they had grown, reproduced, and spread throughout her body, carried by her veins and arteries into new battlefields of flesh, blood, and bone. The war had begun. And the invaders were winning.

It was 9:15 P.M.

Overwhelmed by shock and stress, Jessie Frank retired to her bedroom for a short nap. She fell asleep quickly. Her breathing was slow and steady. Her mind was blank. But the cells of her body still buzzed with activity . . .

In her veins and arteries, a troop of white blood cells attacked a squad of dark microbes—and lost.

In her bones, the unseen enemy penetrated the porous walls of calcium—and like an undercover spy, crept into the marrow.

In her liver, spleen, and kidneys, living barricades of human tissues tried to block a dangerous assault—and failed.

And in every layer of her skin, the epidermal cells prepared for the final battle—one that could bring the organisms' war screaming to the surface . . .

It was a Battle of the Flesh.

The enemy gathered its forces in the bloodstream. Then, following the flow to its farthest reaches, the dark microbes broke through the veins that fed the deepest layers of skin—and began to spread out. The skin cells resisted, but the enemy was too strong. They conquered without mercy. They killed without remorse. And swiftly, without warning, they claimed their territories . . .

The left elbow. The right ankle. The lower neck.

These regions no longer belonged to the life form called Jessie Frank.

They were the spoils of war, the genetic victory of the monsters who spawned her.

It was 10:26 P.M.

Jessie Frank was about to wake up . . .

And meet the enemy face-to-face.

Sara Watkins gripped the steering wheel of her family's station wagon and turned onto Bloom Street. Eddie sat next to her. Neither one of them spoke. They were thinking . . .

About Grandfather Frank.

And monsters.

Sara pulled up in front of Eddie's house and turned off the motor. Then she looked over and sighed.

"I still don't get it," said Eddie. "Why would Grandfather Frank want to make more monsters?"

Sara shrugged. "I don't know. To get revenge on all of us?"

Eddie shook his head. "He has no reason to hate us. If anything, we helped him accomplish his goal. We resurrected Josh."

Sara stared out at the streetlights. They seemed so bright, but not bright enough to conquer the darkness. "Maybe he's after Josh," she said. "He fell to his death when Josh attacked him."

Eddie leaned back against the car seat. "Maybe the fall crushed his brain and he went crazy."

"You'd have to be crazy to make a monster," said Sara.

"Oh, yeah?" said Eddie, winking. "Look who's talking."

"Good point."

Sara turned and looked across Bloom Street at the town and the lake. Tiny lights twinkled in the distance. So many houses—with so many potential victims.

Sara shivered.

"Are you cold?" Eddie asked.

"Freezing," she answered.

Eddie swallowed. "Wanna snuggle for warmth?"

Sara looked over and smirked. Eddie was so cute, with his big brown eyes and long fluffy hair and awkward boyish charm. "Okay," she said.

They slid closer together on the car seat. Then Eddie slipped his arm up and around her shoulders. "There," he said, cuddling up to her. "Warmer?"

"Yes," she said in a soft voice. It felt so good, so comforting, to be in Eddie's arms. It reminded her of all the times she snuggled with Josh—all the times he held her and kissed her . . .

Josh . . .

Suddenly she was overwhelmed with emotion. Her heart was aching with pain—because she was torn between two lovers, torn between life and death itself.

Get a grip, Sara, she told herself. You have enough things on your mind now—like Grandfather Frank.

"I wonder where he is . . . right now," she whispered, resting her head against Eddie's shoulder and gazing out at the lights of Thunder Lake.

Eddie took a deep breath. "Well, if he's making monsters, he's going to need electricity and equipment . . . all the stuff we used to resurrect Josh in . . ." He stopped and looked at Sara.

"The old mill!"

They both said it at the same time.

"Of course!" Sara cried. "Everything he needs is right there in the mill! It's a working laboratory! Why didn't we think of it before? It all makes sense."

"That's probably how Baskerville escaped," said Eddie. "I bet Grandfather Frank let him loose and sent him home so we wouldn't go out there."

Sara sat up and turned the ignition key of the car.

"What are you doing?" said Eddie, alarmed.

"I'm going out there. What do you think I'm doing?"

"Wait, wait!" Eddie reached over and turned off the ignition. "I can't go now. My parents gave me strict orders to be in by eleven o'clock. You know how mad they are at me, ever since I wrecked the car."

Sara sighed and glared at her friend. "Fine," she said. "Go home. I'm going to check it out for myself."

"Sara, no!"

"Why not?"

"You can't go out there by yourself! It's dangerous! The guy's crazy! He might even have a whole army of monsters! You could get killed, Sara!" Eddie was nearly hysterical, his eyes filled with tears. "I won't let you go out there by yourself! I won't let you!"

Sara was stunned by Eddie's reaction. And she was even more stunned when he threw his arms around her and hugged her and wept.

"Don't you know I love you, Sara?" he gasped. "I love you, and I don't want to lose you."

Sara was shocked. She had never seen Eddie cry like this. It was almost as if a dam of emotions had broken inside of him, spilling out every feeling of love and passion and terror that had been pent up for months.

She held him and stroked his long black hair.

Then slowly she lifted his head—and kissed him on the lips.

Eddie wept as she kissed him, overwhelmed by her touch. He had never imagined love could be like this. So powerful. So intense. And he couldn't believe it was happening to *him*. Eddie Perez. The Puerto Rican computer nerd without a friend in the world. Love was never a part of his dreams. It was something too rare and magical for someone like him. Love was reserved for the popular and beautiful ones. Not for Eddie Perez.

But now Sara Watkins was holding him in her arms and kissing his lips and whispering in his ear . . .

"I love you, Eddie."

And for the first time in his life, Eddie Perez felt truly loved.

But he couldn't stop crying. It was kind of embarrassing. The hot salty tears were flowing down his face, and Sara was kissing them, one by one, assuring him that he had nothing to be embarrassed about.

"Promise me you won't do anything crazy," he sobbed. "Promise me you won't go and get yourself killed."

Sara's eyes glistened under the streetlights. "I promise," she whispered.

Then they sat back in the seat of the car, hugging and staring out across the black waters of Thunder Lake. After a few moments, Sara lifted her head and sighed.

"We'll go to the mill tomorrow," she said. "Together."

Eddie squeezed her shoulder. "What do you suppose is happening out there? What do you think he's doing with all those dead bodies?"

"I don't know," Sara whispered. "But just the thought of it makes my skin crawl."

Jessie opened her eyes.

At first, she didn't know where she was. Her bedroom seemed like a foreign land, dark and mysterious. She hardly recognized it. She felt like an intruder, a stranger in a strange land—as if she had died and come back to life in a different body. Then, blinking her eyes and scratching her neck, she began to feel human again.

"I hate naps," she grumbled to herself. "I feel dizzy . . . yucky . . . gross . . ." Slowly she sat up in bed and swung her feet to the floor.

That's when she noticed her ankle . . .

And the signs of decay.

As soon as she saw the dark splotches on her skin, her heart started pounding in her chest. Her breathing grew short. Her brain screamed in horror.

"Nooo!"

She crossed her legs to get a closer look—and gasped when she saw the gray patches of dead flesh that circled her ankle. The skin was dry, scaly . . .

Rotting.

"Nooo!"

She cried out in terror, her mind reeling . . .

I'm not a monster, I'm not rotting away, I'm not!

But the facts were staring her in the face. The gruesome signs of grave rot were there, on her leg, eating her up, tainting her flesh.

Frantically, Jessie searched her body for other patches of dead skin. Her legs, her hips, her arms . . .

She screamed.

Her left elbow was hideous—even worse than her ankle. The gray, rotting flesh had begun to bubble and peel away, and a sickly swirl of tiny dark dots seemed to be creeping up her arm.

"I'm rotting away," she whispered in disbelief.

Her legs were shaky when she stood up to look at her face in the mirror. And she was afraid her legs would collapse beneath her when she saw her reflection.

There, at the base of her neck . . .

Another spot of death.

Jessie stared at the ugly gray patch, then picked at it with her finger. A tiny flake broke away and floated to the floor. She watched it fall, her mind twisting and turning and losing control. But she didn't faint or collapse.

Instead, she stared at herself in the mirror—and cried and whispered over and over and over again . . .

"I'm a monster. I'm a monster. I'm a monster."

13

Whispers of the Dead

From the diary of Jessie Frank . . .

There is no escape from the truth.

My mother and father were monsters. My brother, Josh, is a monster. And now I, Jessie Frank, am a monster, too.

The curse of Frankenstein will never die. The dead will not stay buried. Even now, as I lie here on my bed, I swear I can hear their whispers. The voices of the dead are calling out to me, beckoning me . . . I'm probably losing my mind. It's just the wind. A storm is brewing outside—I feel it in my bones. But I refuse to surrender. I'll close my eyes and wait for it to pass. I want to fall asleep . . .

Because sleep is the closest thing to death.

The Frank family mansion was dark and silent. It stood alone on the edge of the lake, a fortress against the wind that came rushing across the icy black water. Every gothic arch, every gable and window, every plank, beam, and stone felt the wind's fury. Lashing. Screaming. Tormenting.

The wind was not alone.

Tonight, it carried rain clouds on its back—and thunder and lightning in its pockets. Tonight, it would unleash these forces in a wild and reckless display of nature's fury. Tonight, it would punish the earth and challenge the heavens.

But that's not all.

The wind had a secret weapon tonight. It had the sound to match its fury, an unearthly chorus of voices . . .

They floated on the wind like boats on a river—an eerie duet of ghastly whispers, drifting and wailing. They called out from the shores of the lake, then rippled across the grass and trees, gaining strength and substance as they moved closer and closer to the Frank family mansion.

They were the whispers of the dead . . .

And they'd come home at last.

The creature shifted in his cage—and opened his eyes.

Mother? Father?

He lifted his head and looked around the room. The basement was dark and empty. The creature was alone.

No Mother. No Father.

It must have been a dream.

The creature lifted one of his massive arms and rubbed his eyes. His fingers touched the scars on his face, then pulled away in horror. The creature did not like to touch his face. It reminded him of how ugly he was. Ugly and dead. A monster.

The creature felt a twinge of pain.

It was a different kind of pain than being struck with a piece of wood, or having stitches ripped from his flesh. It was an invisible pain. In his heart.

And it hurt even more than the other kind of pain.

Slowly he turned his head and stared at the broken guitar in the corner. The basement was dark, almost black, but his glowing eyes could see it clearly. A tangle of wood and strings. All that remained of his music.

Never again, he thought. Music dead. Like me.

Tears filled the creature's eyes. Ever since he woke up, he felt like crying. He didn't know why. Maybe it was the dream he had. The dream about his mother and father.

They were calling to him.

Crying out. Whispering his name.

Now the creature could not even remember his name. It was lost with the dream. Lost forever.

He closed his eyes and tried to think. What was his name? What did they call him when he was alive? What was the name of the girl with yellow hair . . . the girl that he loved?

Sara.

Yes, that was it. Sara. Beautiful Sara, who gave him the ring and told him that she loved him.

The creature reached into his pocket and pulled out the gold family ring. It glistened in the darkness, like a beacon. So pretty. Like Sara. The creature smiled through his tears. He kissed the ring with dry, cracked lips.

Then he tried to remember his name.

He was a teenage boy once. A handsome boy. Smart, too. And he played music. That he remembered. But what was his name? Who was he, really?

The creature closed his eyes and listened to the wind howling outside the mansion. It sounded like someone crying. Then he heard a sound, like a breathy whisper, wailing over the screams of the wind . . .

"*Josh* . . ."

He opened his eyes and listened again.

"*Joshua* . . ."

And the tears began to flow down his twisted, scarred face.

Because it was *his* name, floating on the wind, penetrating the walls of the house. His name. Josh. Joshua. There, he heard it again.

"*Joshua* . . ."

The haunting sound echoed in the night. It wasn't a dream. It was real. Someone was calling to him, crying out his name. "*Josh* . . ."

The creature stood up in his cage and grasped the steel bars. He could feel the storm coming, feeding him, giving him strength. And he could hear the voices of the dead.

"*Come, Josh . . . come.*"

It was a voice he knew. A voice he hadn't heard in years and years.

It was the voice of his mother . . .

And she wanted him to come.

Grabbing and pulling the bars as hard as he could, the creature growled with rage. He felt the steel bend in his hands, surrendering to his strength. And soon, the bars were gaping open . . .

And the creature was free.

First, he staggered out into the basement. Then, he stomped up the stairs, taking two at a time. As he crossed the hall toward the front door, he heard his mother's voice again—and something else . . .

Growling.

It was Baskerville. The dog he loved all his life. The dog he strangled after death. The big black hound stood at the base of the stairs, growling at his former master. He dug his paws into the floor, sniffing the air—and smelling danger.

The thing that used to be Josh reached for the doorknob and hesitated. Baskerville wanted to stop him. Something was wrong. But the creature didn't care. His mother was calling to him, calling him by name . . .

"*Joshua . . .*"

The creature couldn't resist any longer. He swung open the mansion door and stepped outside. Baskerville barked and jumped, but the creature slammed the door before he could follow.

Then Josh was outside. Alone. With the darkness. With the wind . . .

With his mother and father.

"*Josh.*"

He looked up at the two corpses standing before him.

His mother was tall and thin, a half-rotted skeleton with wild black hair streaked with wriggling worms and mold. Her long bony hands were stretched out in front of her like two naked tree branches. Her fingernails were like claws.

His father was monstrously tall and horribly decayed. His giant, powerful arms hung like rotting meat by his side. He glared at his son with hatred and love, his deep-set eyes burning like coals.

Josh was too afraid to move.

He was the one who dug them up from their graves and who freed them from the prisons of their caskets. But he was also the one who destroyed them at the mill, who shoved their rotted bodies onto the waterwheel and watched them plunge over the edge of the dam. Somehow they survived.

Did they still love him?

Could anyone love the thing that used to be Josh?

Standing on the edge of the porch, the creature watched his parents through his tears—and waited for their reaction. The wind screamed over their heads, blowing his mother's hair like the shredded sails of a ghost ship. Her eyes glowed in the darkness. And her mouth opened in a grotesque mockery of a smile . . .

"Come, Josh," she said in a dead, cracked voice.

Then his mother and father turned and walked away down the stone path of the mansion.

Josh watched the two ghostly figures fade into the night. The image shifted and blurred as he wiped the tears from his eyes—and followed in his parents' footsteps.

He spotted them on the edge of the lake, their grisly silhouettes shimmering against the water. They were walking slowly. Every move they made looked jagged—and painful. Josh staggered toward them, glancing up at the huge storm clouds gathering overhead.

Where were they taking him? And why?

Soon he saw a dark building in the distance—and his heart was filled with dread.

It was the old mill.

Where Josh was brought back to life.

A shadow of terror crossed Josh's soul. He knew the mill was a bad place. A place filled with chains and knives and lightning and thunder. He didn't want to go there. But he had to follow his mother and father. He had to know why they wanted him to come . . .

For revenge?

Would they push him onto the waterwheel and watch him plunge over the dam?

The creature stopped in his tracks. He saw his father open the door of the mill and step inside. There was light in the building—and a thin shadow. Then his mother stopped in the doorway and turned around.

"*Come, Josh,*" she whispered. "*Come.*"

The door closed—and Josh was left alone in the darkness. The wind shrieked across the lake. He stared up at the clouds and felt the surging power of electricity in the air. The smell of thunder filled his senses— and the promise of lightning fortified his strength.

Yes, he would go inside. Even if they wanted revenge. Even if they wanted to kill him.

Josh was not afraid of death.

He craved it.

So, lunging forward, the creature approached the place of his rebirth, where life and death turned as slowly and surely as the old wooden waterwheel. His footsteps clomped across the wooden boards of the dock. His hand reached out to open the door of the mill.

And the creature stepped inside.

At first, the light seemed too blindingly bright for Josh to see anything at all. Then his eyes adjusted to the glare.

And he flinched when he saw the horrors within . . .

Chained to a huge beam in the corner were the resurrected bodies of Moose and Mike Morgan—two pale, shambling corpses who groaned in misery and glared with empty dead eyes.

On the lab table in the center of the room, the body of Heather Leigh Clark lay under a bloody sheet, her long blond hair flowing over the edge of the table.

And on the far end of the lab, a row of chains rattled against a locked door while an unimaginable beast snarled and snapped from within.

But that wasn't what frightened Josh.

What frightened Josh was the man standing next to a table of scalpels and needles. The man who created his monstrous parents . . .

Grandfather Frank.

The old man was as white as a ghost—and covered with blood. He stared at Josh with wild, blazing eyes, grinning like a hungry animal. His neck was torn and broken but held together with splints of steel and wire. His legs, too, were repaired in the same gruesome way. He leaned back against the table, smiling and twitching. His face trembled with pure madness. And his gnarled, twisted hands gripped a small bloody saw.

"I'm so glad you could join us, Josh," he said in a voice as broken and grisly as his appearance. "Pull up a chair and join the family."

Josh snarled and took a step backward. Grandfather Frank laughed.

"I suggest you do as you're told, Josh," he said. "Or else your closest, dearest friends could meet the same fate as those two."

He pointed at the Morgan brothers in the corner. The monstrous boys cowered in fear and pulled against the chains. They were terrified.

Josh turned to face his parents—but they had walked to the other corner of the room and were now placing chains around their own necks.

"See?" said Grandfather Frank. "Even your mother and father know enough to follow my orders. I can't tolerate a monster who misbehaves." He held up the bloody saw. "The consequences can be very . . . painful."

Josh watched in horror as his parents chained themselves to a massive beam. Then he looked at the Morgan brothers and saw the fear in their eyes. Their foreheads were covered with gashes and scars—as if Grandfather Frank had opened their heads . . .

And cut up their brains.

"I need your help, Josh. That's why I called you here," said the old man, pacing the floor. "Your parents are too weak, and those idiots in the corner are too stupid." He pointed at the Morgans, and they flinched. "I sent them to the mall to kill a beautiful blond girl. But the brain-dead fools grabbed the wrong girl! A silly cheerleader named Heather Leigh Clark!"

Josh glanced at the body on the lab table. Grandfather Frank tried to block his view.

"I wanted to get Sara," he said. "For you, Josh. As a gift."

Josh's heart jumped.

Sara? Dead? Like me?

He opened his mouth and screamed.

"*Nooo!!*"

Grandfather Frank laughed. "Don't worry, Josh. Sara is still alive," he said. "But that could change . . . if you don't follow my orders."

A single tear rolled down Josh's cheek.

"Now, now, don't cry," said Grandfather Frank. "If you help me, Josh, I'll give you anything you want. Think about it. You can have a family again. You can have food and warmth and all the love in the world. Did you hear me, Josh? Love. I can give you *love . . .*"

The word echoed in the creature's brain. It was something from his past, something for the living. He tried to remember this thing called love. He knew it was beautiful and bright. It made him feel glad to be alive. Love. He tried to picture what it looked like, and a single image appeared in his mind . . .

Sara.

The creature closed his eyes and whispered, "*Love . . . ?*"

Grandfather Frank clapped his mangled hands together and laughed.

"Yes, Josh! Love! Love, love, love! Sweet eternal love! Love everlasting!"

He huddled over the corpse on the lab table, stroking her hair, grinning madly.

"And have I got a girl for you!"

14

The Bride

From the secret journal of Professor Frank . . .

Nothing can stop me now.

With the secrets of life and death, I have created a master race of beings who will follow my every command. Like the angels of heaven, they are eternal—and like the demons of hell, they are strong. They are the new children of earth. Frankenstein's children. My children.

Together, we will destroy this useless world of weak and foolish mortals. We will build a new Garden of Eden. And I, as the new god of life and death, will gather my children around me. Then I will tell them to go forth . . .

Be fruitful and multiply.

Heather Leigh Clark was dead.

So she didn't feel the needle piercing her jugular, draining every last drop of human blood from her body. Nor did she feel the blue artificial plasma being pumped into her veins—or the steel bolts being wired into her nervous system through her neck and spinal cord.

Her body was an empty vessel, waiting to be filled. With thunder. With lightning. With life itself.

And tonight, long after midnight, the dead cheer-leader would feel the triumph of science over nature—and the agonies of her own rebirth.

Grandfather Frank leaned over Heather's corpse, attaching wires and cables to the bolts in her neck. He looked up at the thing that used to be Josh—and grinned.

"What do you think, Josh, my boy? Lovely, isn't she? Every bit as lovely as Sara."

The creature stared down at the gruesome sight of Heather's body. His lower lip quivered.

"I know, she's a little damaged," said Grandfather Frank. "Because those *half-wits* were too rough!" he snapped at the Morgan boys in the corner.

The reanimated brothers jumped. Mike Morgan, the smaller monster, pulled back on his chain and lifted his head and whimpered. A trickle of drool streamed down his splotchy yellow chin. Moose, the larger monster, tried to back off, but he was too bloated and clumsy. His massive gray body looked like it would burst if you stuck him with a pin. When he reached up to scratch the gaping scar on his forehead, a tiny piece of brain broke off and fell to the floor. Moose picked it up and ate it.

Josh looked back at the lab table and grunted.

"Don't worry, Josh. I'll fix her up for you," said Grandfather Frank, threading a needle. "She'll be beautiful, just wait and see. I'll simply clean up the mess . . . like this . . . and sew it up . . . like that . . ." The old man cursed under his breath. "These blasted hands of mine! Now look what I've done!"

Josh stared in horror at the body of Heather Leigh Clark. What was Grandfather Frank doing to her? He was making her ugly, turning her into a monster . . .

Like me.

His eyes filled with tears, and something stirred in his heart—a loneliness as dark and vast as the storm clouds gathering outside the mill. He reached into his pocket and clutched the gold family ring he had given to Sara.

"It's time," said Grandfather Frank, staring up at the open tower. A rumble of thunder shook the old mill. "It's going to be a beautiful storm." He turned back to his creation on the table. "And she's going to be a beautiful bride!"

A flash of lightning streaked across the sky. Josh looked up through the broken windows of the tower—and held his breath.

Grandfather Frank ran back and forth in the lab, turning knobs and dials, hooking up cables, and plunging a needle into the base of Heather's spine. His eyes blazed with excitement. His hands trembled with anticipation.

"It's coming! It's coming!" he cried. "Lightning! The purest form of electricity!" He turned to the other monsters, chained to the beams. "I should never have used man-made electricity to create you . . . you pathetic beasts!"

The storm raged, and the monsters howled with fear.

Josh moved away toward the wall. The storm frightened him—as much as it gave him strength.

Suddenly a crashing boom of thunder exploded over-head, and a heavy gush of rain blasted the roof and walls of the mill. The electric lights flickered, the darkness slashed with alternating shadows and lightning.

Josh groaned and shut his eyes.

And Grandfather Frank roared with laughter. "Yes! Yes!" he cried. "The storm is here!"

Limping on thin, splinted legs, the old man crossed the lab to a giant iron wheel. He gripped it tightly with his twisted hands and turned it slowly. Four heavy chains clanked and rattled in the air—and lifted the body of Heather Leigh Clark up, up to the tower . . .

Up to the heavens.

Josh squinted his eyes against the lightning's glare and watched the lab table rise. All he could see was the shape of the table—and the cheerleader's long blond hair flowing over the edge.

Then—another crash of lightning and thunder—and Heather's hair was twisting and writhing like a nest of snakes.

There was electricity everywhere. Josh could feel it. In the air. In the body up in the tower. In his own muscles and veins. It was like life itself—hard, cruel, and painful.

He tilted back his head and roared.

Because he hated electricity.

He hated life.

Suddenly the heavens opened up—and the storm unleashed its ultimate fury. A jagged claw of light-ning reached down from the clouds, searching for something to strike.

And that something was Heather Leigh Clark.

A blinding flash illuminated the whole mill—as the long finger of nature's light penetrated the body on the table. The deafening explosion of thunder filled the night, a shattering screech that sounded almost human. Like a woman's scream.

Then everything was darkness.

A cold silence fell over the mill. No one moved or spoke. Only the wind dared to whisper as it blew the storm gently across the lake. Time seemed to stand still.

Then suddenly, in the darkness of the mill, a single chilling sound pierced the veil of silence . . .

The sound of weeping.

And it was coming from up in the tower—from Heather's corpse . . .

She was crying.

Grandfather Frank was ecstatic.

"She's alive! Alive!"

The old man laughed and cheered as he limped to the fuse box and turned on the lights. Josh squinted his eyes. He looked up at the tower and saw the teenage girl's hair floating back and forth over the edge of the lab table. It looked like fire . . .

Josh did not like fire.

Fire burned. Fire hurt.

He leaned back against the wall and trembled as Grandfather Frank turned the iron wheel, lowering the lab table slowly toward the floor. As Heather's body descended, the old man hummed a haunting tune . . .

"Here Comes the Bride."

Josh dug his huge fingers into the wooden boards of the wall. Splinters pierced his flesh, but he did not cry out. He was frozen with fear—and burning with curiosity.

He remembered the word that Grandfather Frank had spoken to him . . .

Love.

And he remembered the way he used to hold Sara in his arms, the way they looked into each other's eyes, the way they kissed . . .

Love.

Could it be possible? Could the yellow-haired thing on the table ever love a thing like himself?

Josh's eyes glistened as he watched the sheet-covered body fall from heaven to earth. Like an angel. The chains rattled and clanked, lowering the girl's body slowly to the floor.

Finally, she reached the ground.

And Grandfather Frank staggered to the table and gasped. "Perfection!" Moving swiftly, he disconnected the cables and wires on her neck and the straps on her ankles and wrists. Then, grabbing a fresh white sheet, he wrapped her torso and tied the ends of the linen under her arms.

He looked up at Josh and shrugged. "It's not much of a wedding dress, but it'll have to do," he said. "Come, Josh. Step up . . . and meet your bride-to-be."

The creature hesitated. His heart was pounding so hard against his chest, he could feel his stitches pulling on his skin. He was mortified. He felt stupid and ugly.

How could anyone love him?

Slowly he took a step forward, then another. Grandfather Frank was smiling at him, waving him forward with his mangled, bloody hand. "Come meet her, Josh. I made her for you . . ."

Then he tilted the lab table to an upright position—and revealed his latest creation.

"The Bride of Frankenstein!"

The old man cackled with glee and waited for Josh's reaction. The creature stared down at his mate with a look of childlike fascination. His cold dead eyes gleamed . . .

Because Heather was every bit as monstrous as he was.

She was truly the Bride of Frankenstein.

Her hair was a tangled mass of yellow and green, twisting and floating in the air like an electric tornado. Her skin was spotted and streaked with dusty gray splotches of lavender and pink. Her face was stretched tight over the bones of her skull and pulled out of shape by a patchwork of stitches. Her lips were red with blood. And her eyes were like two brilliant blue stones—hard and cold . . .

She was hideous.

Like Josh.

He trembled under her gaze, then turned away in fear. He looked across the room at his mother and father. They stared back at him with sunken eyes filled with hope and dread—the parents of the groom. The chains rattled against their necks as they strained to see the bride.

"Take her hand, Josh," said Grandfather Frank.

Josh hesitated—then reached out, forgetting the tiny gold object resting in his massive palm . . .

The Frank family ring.

"You have a ring!" cried the old man. "How lovely! Slip it over her finger, Josh! Show her you love her!"

Heather's unearthly blue eyes glowed when she saw the gold ring in his hand. She opened her bloodred mouth and hissed. Then her right hand, like a claw of lightning, lashed out for the glittering band of gold.

Josh quickly pulled his hand away, slipping the ring into his pocket. He couldn't give it to Heather, his monstrous bride . . .

It belonged to Sara.

The thing that used to be Heather screeched in rage—and attacked him with her razor-sharp fingernails. Josh staggered backward as she dug into the stitches on his face, clawing and ripping, hissing and screaming . . .

This was not what Grandfather Frank had promised. This was not the thing called love. It was hate at first sight.

"No! Stop it!" cried Grandfather Frank. "You're man and wife! You're made for each other!"

The gruesome honeymooners, locked in battle, spun around and crashed into a table of scalpels and needles. Heather's face was inches away from Josh's. He could see the hatred burning in her eyes. Then the dead cheerleader bared her teeth, hissed and screamed . . .

"Ugly! Ugly! Ugly!"

Her voice was a loud, grotesque screech that rang in Josh's ears—and pierced his artificial heart. Suddenly he was crying, the hot tears scalding the open scars on his face. The truth of her words scorched his soul . . .

He was ugly.

How could anyone love something so ugly?

Pushing the she-creature away, Josh staggered to his feet and ran to the door. Heather pulled herself up to a catlike stance, her wild mane of hair bristling with sparks. She bared her blood-soaked teeth and hissed at him.

"*Ugly!*"

Josh turned away in shame and horror. He wrenched the door open with a loud bang, then stood in the doorway glaring at Heather, the Morgan boys, his mother and father—and the man who had created them.

Grandfather Frank was furious.

"Where do you think you're going, Josh?" he howled. His head twitched from side to side, straining against the steel splints. "I created you! You're mine!"

Josh stared at the old man with bitterness and disgust. Then he opened his mouth and roared like a wild beast.

"If you run out on me, I'll get you, Josh!" shouted the old man. "I'll get you . . . and your little friends, too! I'll send my monsters after them, one by one. Sara, Jessie, and Eddie will be mine! Frankenstein's children!!"

Josh roared again, then charged at the old man, smashing into his chest and sending him sprawling across the laboratory floor. Then the monstrous boy turned and walked back to the door. Heather swiped at him with her lightning-fast fingernails, slicing his leg as he passed. Josh ignored her.

Grandfather Frank raised his head on his broken neck and spit out a bloody tooth.

Then he looked up to see Josh walk out the door of the mill—and vanish into the night.

"I'll get you," he muttered under his breath. "I'll get all of you!"

The old man pulled himself up, leaned against the lab table, and reached into his pocket—for a set of keys. Then he limped from one creature to the other, unlocking the chains that bound them.

"Get up, you miserable creatures!" he cried. "Get up and get to work!"

The Morgan boys cowered in fear as he pulled the shackles from their necks.

"I want them all!" the old man babbled. "Josh, Sara, Jessie, Eddie! I want their dead bodies! And I want them tonight!!"

He tore the chains from the zombie-thin necks of the mother and father.

"Get up and go! Into the night!" he bellowed. "Rob the graves in the cemetery! Raid the morgue! And bring back the bodies of those ungrateful children!"

The monsters rose to their feet. Heather crept to the doorway and looked out, her eyes sparkling with hatred. The Morgan boys lumbered after her, and the parents followed.

Then Grandfather Frank staggered toward the small locked door at the end of the room. The beast within snarled and snapped and threw itself against the door, jolting the chains.

"You, too," the old man whispered, turning the key in the lock—and freeing the monstrosity inside. It burst through the door and dashed across the room, pushing through the startled group of monsters. Then it ran outside and howled at the moon.

"Go, my children, go!" shouted the old man, foaming at the mouth. "Turn the night into a nightmare!!"

Then he cackled like a mad fiend . . .

And watched his children scatter in the dark.

15

Invasion of the Body Snatchers

From the diary of Sara Watkins . . .

Sometimes the human mind chooses to forget things that are too painful to remember. But as long as I live, I will never be able to erase the memories of that terrible night.

From the moment I decided to resurrect Josh, I tried to anticipate every horror before it happened. But this time, I didn't see it coming. This time, it shocked me out of my sleep—and screamed in my ear like the sirens that soon echoed across Thunder Lake.

It was a night to remember, a night of madness, terror, and chaos . . .

And it was only a shadow of things to come.

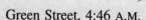

Green Street, 4:46 A.M.

In a small bedroom on the ground floor of a red brick house, Sara Watkins shifted in her sleep.

In her dreams, she was about to be crowned Homecoming Queen. All of her loved ones were gathered around her, smiling and clapping and snapping photos. The flashbulbs blinded her vision as she waved to the crowds. Her parents and grandparents looked so proud. Jessie and Eddie were there, too, cheering her on. Then she blinked her eyes—and everything changed.

Jessie was a monster—her flesh rotting and peeling before her eyes. Sara cried out to Eddie, but he, too, was transforming. A pair of shiny steel bolts ripped through the flesh of his neck. Sara tried to scream for help. She ran to the edge of the stage and froze— because every single person in the crowd had turned into a monster. Her parents and grandparents howled like animals, their hair littered with worms, their skin slashed with stitches.

Then Grandfather Frank appeared beside her, hold- ing a gleaming crown of razor-sharp scalpels—and he was trying to thrust the fatal crown on Sara's head.

Sara screamed and screamed. The monsters swarmed around the stage, reaching for her with long skeletal hands . . .

And then Sara woke up—but not from fear . . .

Someone was banging on her bedroom window.

Sitting up and climbing out of bed, she raced across the room to look out the window. As soon as she saw the dark outline of a towering silhouette, she knew who it was.

Josh . . .

Without hesitating, Sara flung open her bedroom window. "Josh!" she whispered. "What are you doing here?"

Then she saw the tears in his eyes—and terror on his face.

"What's wrong?" she asked, wishing he could answer. She reached for the monster's hand, but he backed away and moaned. His arms were stretched out in front of him. His hands were beckoning her forward.

"Okay, I'm coming, Josh! Wait right there!" She turned and frantically dressed herself in jeans, a jacket, and sneakers. Then she tiptoed through the house and crept out the back door.

Josh was waiting for her by the side of the house. His massive head turned back and forth, his haunted eyes scanning the night. Sara approached him slowly.

"What's wrong, Josh?" she whispered. "What are you looking for?"

Suddenly he grunted in fear and grabbed her hand, pulling her into the shadows. Sara squealed with surprise, and Josh slapped his huge gray hand over her mouth. He was trembling. Sara had never seen him so frightened. What was he afraid of? Why was he staring off into the distance?

She looked up—and saw it . . .

A shimmering ball of sparks came rolling out of the darkness. It glistened and turned—and stepped under the streetlight. It wasn't a ball of sparks. It was the lightning-struck hair of a hideous she-creature. A man-made thing with stitches on her face, blood on her lips, and hate in her eyes.

It was Heather Leigh Clark . . .

And she was heading right for them.

Bloom Street, 4:58 A.M.

Eddie Perez couldn't sleep, so he got up and walked to the kitchen to make himself a peanut butter sandwich. When he saw the face in the window, he jumped—then laughed at himself for being such a wimp. It was only his reflection.

You're not a wimp anymore, he reminded himself, admiring his long wavy hair in the glass.

He sat down at the table to eat his sandwich—and thought about how much he'd changed since he met Sara. It was more than just a new look and hairstyle. It was his attitude that had changed. After robbing a morgue and raising the dead, high school seemed like a piece of cake. Now Eddie Perez was confident and strong—not just another nerd for the school jocks to bully around.

And anyway, Moose Morgan—the biggest bully of all—was dead.

That's what Eddie was thinking when he heard the trash cans clatter and fall on the back porch.

He stopped chewing and turned his head. What was that? A prowler?

The old Eddie would have been too chicken to check it out. But the new Eddie was strong and self-assured.

Yeah, right, he thought.

Slowly, his heart pounding, Eddie stood up and crept toward the back door. First, he peeked out the window. Nothing. Then he opened the door and stepped outside, pulling his bathrobe tighter around him.

And that's when the resurrected corpse of Moose Morgan grabbed him by the throat . . .

And dragged him into the night.

The County Morgue, 5:03 A.M.

Nurse Nancy hated the graveyard shift, especially in

a morgue. It was just too ghoulish for words. The last time she worked here, she spotted two kids walking out with a bag full of dismembered limbs. She called security immediately, but they laughed at her—told her she was crazy!

Of course, the next day everyone threw a fit when they noticed the missing body parts. Served them right, thought Nurse Nancy. She'd have the last laugh.

So tonight, as the two rotting zombies passed her desk with a bundle of arms and legs and organs, the usually competent Nurse Nancy kept her mouth shut.

"I didn't see a thing," she'd tell them.

The Frank Family Mansion, 5:15 A.M.

It was the sound of howling that woke Jessie Frank.

She shifted and rolled over in bed, then opened her eyes and whispered, "Baskerville?" She waited and listened—and heard it again . . .

It started with a low growl and escalated to a fever pitch, echoing throughout the house. It was definitely Baskerville. Jessie recognized his howl. And it seemed to be coming from the entry hall of the mansion.

"Did you see a kitty-cat, Basker-baby?" she groaned as she sat up in bed. The dog's howl pierced her ears, and she winced. "Okay, I'm coming, Robo-pooch. I'm coming!"

She put on her slippers and robe and walked down the hall to the top of the stairs. From there, she could see Baskerville scratching at the front door. "Stupid dog," she mumbled as she climbed down the stairs and crossed the entry hall. "What's gotten into you?"

She reached down to grab his collar, but the hound turned and snapped at her, then sniffed at the door, whimpering and pleading.

Jessie shrugged her shoulders. "Okay, puppy, I'll let you out." She fumbled with the doorknob and flung open the door.

Baskerville barked and dashed out into the front yard, stopping on the stone path where he sniffed the air and growled. Jessie stepped out onto the front porch, watching him. "What do you see, Baskerville? A rabbit? A cat? A squirrel?" She rubbed her eyes and stared into the night.

Everything was wet and foggy, as if there'd been a big rainstorm. Jessie was surprised she didn't feel the storm in her blood. Maybe it didn't affect her this time. With a mixed sense of hope and dread, she looked down at her arms . . .

And saw the ugly gray rot.

It had doubled in size, crawling up both arms now, like a vile breed of fungus.

Jessie gasped in horror—and looked up to see something charging out of the fog. It ran on four legs down the stone path of the mansion, snapping and lunging straight for Baskerville. It looked like a dog. But it wasn't.

Jessie screamed as the beast attacked.

Because the doglike creature had a human head.

And not just any head. It was the head of the original Frankenstein monster, and it had been grafted onto the body of a giant attack dog—the dog that was beheaded in Thunder Lake Cemetery. Jessie watched in shock as the grotesque monstrosity snarled and sunk its teeth into Baskerville's neck, grazing the dog's steel bolts and setting off sparks.

"Noooo!!"

Jessie screamed as the two beasts battled for their lives. They clawed and snapped, growled and bit each other in fury, tumbling and turning on the stone path. Jessie couldn't take her eyes off that horrible face— the grisly monster's head covered with stitches and scars. Its eyes were glowing in the darkness, burning with hate. It was truly a demon from hell.

The sight was so shocking to behold, Jessie never noticed the figure standing behind her on the porch . . .

Until it grabbed her in its arms.

And tried to kiss her.

Jessie struggled as a moldy pair of lips pressed against her cheek. Pulling away in horror, she tried to focus on the splotchy yellow face, the gashes and scars, the cold dead eyes. Then she screamed— screamed and fought for her life—when she realized who it was . . .

Mike Morgan.

The boy who died on his first date with Jessie Frank had risen from the grave.

And he wanted to give her another kiss.

Green Street, 5:32 A.M.

Sara stood in the bushes and watched the two creatures fighting on the lawn.

The corpse of Heather Leigh Clark slashed Josh's face with her fingernails and shoved him to the ground.

Josh cried out in pain. Then Heather began to crawl toward Sara, hissing like a snake.

Sara looked around desperately for a weapon. She couldn't believe this was happening. She was completely unprepared for the resurrection of Heather Leigh Clark. If Josh hadn't attacked the dead cheerleader on sight, Sara would probably be dead herself.

She grabbed a lawn rake that was lying in the grass—and swung it at the rampaging she-creature.

Heather hissed and backed off, then prepared for another attack.

But Sara was ready this time. She swung the rake through the air—and slammed it against Heather's face. The she-devil howled and fell backward. Then she was really mad. She dug her feet into the grass and pounced on Sara like a wildcat.

But Josh had grabbed her ankle. He pulled hard, and Heather Leigh Clark was dragged away. Sara threw the rake at Heather and pulled herself free. She turned and looked at Josh. His eyes burned with urgency.

"*Go . . .*," he growled. "*Run, Sa . . . ra!*"

Sara scrambled to her feet and started running blindly across the yard and down the street. She didn't know where she was running—but she knew she had to get away fast.

Heather Leigh Clark knew where she lived.

Sara's feet pounded on the concrete of Green Street—and the sound was echoed by another pair of footsteps.

I hope that's you, Josh, she thought. And not . . .

Heather grabbed Sara by her hair, stopping her in her tracks.

Sara tried to scream, but she couldn't. The last thing she felt was Heather's clawlike hands wrapping around her body . . .

And dragging her away.

Main Street, 5:41 A.M.

The night sky turned gray over the town of Thunder Lake. But the coming of daylight brought no hope to Eddie Perez . . .

The monstrous corpse of Moose Morgan carried the boy, kicking and screaming, down Main Street itself— but no one seemed to hear him. It was still too early in the morning.

Somebody help me, Eddie thought in vain. Somebody, please, wake up and help me!

But as the gruesome, hulking creature dragged him toward the lake, Eddie knew no one was going to rescue him. He was going to have to get out of this one by himself.

So he opened his mouth—and sunk his teeth into the dead football player's arm.

Moose roared.

And dropped him on the street.

In a flash, Eddie was up and running. He could hear Moose coming after him, howling with rage. Eddie's heart pounded in his chest as he dashed up the street, turned the corner, and scampered up and over a tall iron fence . . .

Into the cemetery.

Thunder Lake Cemetery, 5:51 A.M.

When Jessie opened her eyes, she thought she was dreaming.

There were gravestones everywhere, as far as she could see. And her mother and father were clawing at the earth, digging up bodies.

Slowly Jessie turned her head and looked up. She was lying in the arms of Mike Morgan, who stared down at her like a lovesick ghoul, licking his lips and drooling. His brains were pushing against the stitches on his forehead. And his yellow, stained mouth was moving closer and closer—trying to kiss her.

Jessie screamed.

The two grave-robbing zombies looked up in shock, then staggered to their feet. Even though they'd become the slaves of Grandfather Frank, the long-dead parents couldn't ignore their daughter's cries. So they attacked.

Jessie went rolling onto the grass as the two skeletal monsters grabbed Mike Morgan by the throat—and threw him into the air. He landed on a gravestone with a sickening thud. Then Jessie screamed again as someone scooped her up into his arms—and pulled her away.

"Eddie!" Jessie gasped. "What are you doing here?"

The tall boy pushed his hair out of his eyes and pulled her out of sight behind a mausoleum. "I'm running away from monsters," he whispered. "Same as you. Look!"

He pointed across the cemetery. Jessie squinted her eyes in the morning fog—and saw Sara struggling in the arms of a blondhaired creature with gleaming eyes and bloodstained lips. "It's Heather!" Jessie cried. "Grandfather Frank's turned the head cheerleader into a monster!"

Eddie smirked. "She was always a monster. But now she's a killer, too. Come on!"

And with that, Eddie dashed across the cemetery and charged at Heather's corpse. But he never made it. Something tackled his legs and bit his thigh . . .

It was a dog with a monster's head.

And it was trying to rip out Eddie's throat. Eddie pushed the creature away, his face inches from the gray rotted flesh and burning eyes. He could even smell the monster's breath—it was like a grave that had been opened after two hundred years.

Suddenly the snarling demon was knocked off of him—by Baskerville. The two beasts rolled across the ground, snapping and snarling in a demonic dog-fight.

Jessie ran to help Eddie—and tripped on a grave-stone. When she looked up, her gruesome mother and father were standing over her, reaching out for her. She screamed.

But her screams were no match for Sara's.

The lightning-charged corpse of Heather Leigh Clark pinned Sara against a tall marble tomb— and tried to claw her heart out. The sharp finger-nails tore through Sara's jacket, slashing her skin. Pulling her hand free, Sara managed to haul off and punch her in the face. A stream of blue liquid trickled from Heather's nose. The she-creature howled—and doubled the strength and fury of her attack.

Suddenly, out of nowhere, Josh came running out of the fog and tackled Heather to the ground. Sara gasped with relief and fell back against the tomb, watching as Josh and Heather rolled across the graveyard, roaring like animals.

All hell had broken loose.

With tears in her eyes, Sara scanned the cemetery. Baskerville was fighting an unearthly thing with four legs and a monster's head. Eddie was trying to pull Jessie away from her zombie parents. Moose and Mike Morgan were shambling over the graves, looking for someone to attack. And Josh and Heather Leigh Clark were locked in immortal combat.

It was an all-out war between the living and the dead.

And Sara was afraid the living didn't stand a chance.

Suddenly, as the red morning sun appeared on the horizon, a blast of sirens rang out.

Sara looked toward the front gates of the cemetery—and saw a whole squad of police cars screech to a halt, their red lights flashing in the dull morning light.

"Everybody freeze!" a voice bellowed from a bullhorn. "This is Officer Colker! Nobody move!"

But nobody listened.

Humans and monsters alike scattered to the four corners of the graveyard, scrambling up and over the cemetery fence and disappearing into the woods by the lake.

When the police opened the gates and searched the

grounds, not a soul could be found. Only a few open graves. And traces of blood.

As the sun rose higher in the sky, a strange, peaceful calm fell over the town of Thunder Lake, Pennsylvania.

It was 6:10 A.M.

16

The Point of No Return

From *The Coal County Daily News* . . .

GRAVE ROBBERS STRIKE AGAIN
Unidentified Teens Flee Crime Scene

From *The Weekly Thunder* . . .

INVASION OF THE STUDENT BODY SNATCHERS!
Do Ghouls Rule The School??
Will Homecoming Be Haunted??

From *The Pennsylvania Scandal* . . .

SHOCKING PROOF: DOOMSDAY IS HERE!
Dead Rise and Walk in Pennsylvania Town

The sun rose higher in the sky over Thunder Lake, shimmering off the calm waters—and glaring in Sara's eyes. She sat on the shore and stared blankly at the old mill on the edge of the dam. From a distance, it looked so small and insignificant. Hardly a place where horrors come to life. It was just an old, broken-down building.

But Sara knew better.

Eddie sat next to her, tossing pebbles into the water and studying the ripples as if they held the answers to all their problems. If it were only that simple.

Finally Sara pounded her fist against a rock. "Where is Jessie?" she cried. "I'm worried about her. Where could she have gone?"

Eddie sighed. It was the fifteenth time Sara had asked that question—and still, he had no answer.

"Maybe she went home," he said, tossing another pebble in the water.

Sara shook her head. "But that's the first place the monsters will look. She's smarter than that."

Eddie closed his eyes and groaned. He was exhausted. They had searched the woods for hours looking for Jessie and Baskerville. Their arms were all scratched from thorns and branches. And the only thing they saw was a search party of cops—which made them realize they were being hunted by monsters *and* humans.

So they found a place to hide near the shore. And now they had to figure out what to do next.

Suddenly Sara started to cry.

She hugged her legs and buried her face in her knees, sobbing gently. "Maybe we should just give up," she cried. "And tell the police everything."

Eddie looked up in shock. "But, Sara. We've got to protect Josh. What would they do to him? Put him in jail? Study him like a lab animal? Or would they kill him? And what about Jessie? They'd probably send her to an orphanage or foster home somewhere."

Sara nodded, then looked up with eyes full of tears. "I know," she whispered. "But at least she'd get medical treatment. Don't you see? Our pledge of secrecy could be *killing* her!"

Eddie threw another stone in the lake. He didn't know what to say.

"It's gone too far," said Sara, her voice cracking. "Everything's out of control now. It's bigger than we are."

Eddie frowned. "But we're part of it, Sara. We started this nightmare when we decided to resurrect Josh. And now we're past the point of no return. We started it, and we have to finish it . . . if it's the last thing we do."

Sara looked up at Eddie, surprised by his strength and determination.

"First off, we have to find Jessie," he said, standing up and brushing the dirt off his hands. "Come on, Sara. We have a lot to do."

Sara blinked her eyes—and smiled in spite of herself.

"I love you, Eddie," she said.

Eddie blushed. "What a thing to say when I'm trying to act tough." He kicked the dirt with his shoe and shrugged. "You know I love you, too, Sara. And even if we end up getting killed, I don't regret a thing. Just getting to know you was worth all the trouble."

Sara stood up, threw her arms around him, and kissed him. "I think you're great, Eddie," she whispered.

Then, turning their backs to the lake, they walked off

into the woods, searching for Jessie, Baskerville . . .

And a way to end the curse of Frankenstein.

Jessie felt as if she'd been walking in circles for hours. The woods were so dense, she couldn't find her way out. And she was in such a daze, she couldn't think straight.

Her mind was like a madhouse, and the lunatics had taken over. Gruesome images of monsters filled her brain to the screaming point . . .

Her mother and father. Mike Morgan. Moose Morgan. Heather Leigh Clark. Grandfather Frank. And Josh.

They were monsters, all of them.

And so was Jessie.

She gazed down at the gray rot on her arms—and felt the madness seize her brain.

It wouldn't be long now.

She felt the blood of monsters surging through her veins as she stumbled through the woods, looking for a way out. But she knew she was doomed. The curse had grown too dark and powerful. The end was near.

She had crossed the point of no return.

Maybe I'll die here, she thought. Alone, in the woods.

The thought didn't frighten her. If anything, it was a relief. Even the branches that scratched her face had no effect on her as she staggered onward—toward her destiny.

Suddenly, she heard a rustling in the bushes. Then the sound of growling . . .

"Baskerville! Baby!"

The huge black hound bounded out of the brush and jumped up, licking Jessie's face. She laughed and hugged him and kissed him on the nose. "Am I glad to see you, Basker-pup!" she squealed. "What a good doggie! Do you think you could find our way home? Huh, pooch? Home?"

The big dog barked and wagged his tail. Then, dancing in a circle, he turned and dashed into the woods, stopping and looking back at Jessie. He barked again.

"Okay! Okay! I'm right behind you, buddy!"

It took about fifteen minutes to get out of the woods. And after walking another mile along the lake, Jessie saw her house in the distance . . .

The house of Frankenstein.

The huge, crumbling mansion looked like it had been standing there forever—waiting for Jessie to come home. Its dark, cracked walls held the secrets of her birth. And its blank windows, like eyes, seemed to penetrate her soul.

Jessie managed to smile.

She was coming home—for the last time.

Baskerville barked as he ran up the stone path to the house, then scratched at the door. Jessie felt a strange sense of calm as she walked up behind him and opened the door. She was home at last—and home to stay. She tried not to cry as she walked past the old grandfather clock and climbed the stairs up to her bedroom.

Then, sitting quietly at her desk, she took a piece

of paper and a pen—and started writing her final words . . .

Dear Sara,

I hope you can forgive me.

But I think you'll understand why I did it. Last night, surrounded by the monsters in the cemetery, I knew I had no chance to escape the curse of my birthright. I'm a Frankenstein. My body is rotting more every day. My mind is almost gone. Death is my only hope.

There's one favor I ask of you: hide my body. Take it up into the mountains and bury it, far from the evil clutches of Grandfather Frank and his monstrous children. Please save me from that fate.

And save yourself, Sara.

Forgive yourself for everything you've done. Forgive yourself for resurrecting Josh. And forgive yourself for not being able to save me.

You're my best friend in the world, and I'll love you forever. Keep my love alive in your heart—that's the true secret of eternity. Be sweet to Eddie. He deserves it. And be kind to yourself. Go on with your life, study hard and become a great doctor. But always know that I love you, Sara, like a sister . . .

Even death can't take that away.

> Love you forever,
> Jessie

P.S.—Destroy this note.

Jessie looked up from her desk. She could hear the clock ticking on her nightstand—and the blood pumping through her heart. The madness was there, too, trying to penetrate her brain. But somehow she fought it off.

Just one more note, she told herself. Try to stay sane.

Then, taking another piece of paper, she began to write . . .

Dear Eddie,

I never told you this, but you probably saved my life once.

It was soon after Josh killed himself. I thought I would go crazy with grief. I loved my brother more than anyone—and suddenly he was gone. Then this sweet wonderful boy came into my life, a boy who could talk to me as a true friend and who helped me more than he could ever know. That sweet wonderful boy was you, Eddie. You filled the empty space in my heart after Josh's death. You made me laugh. You gave me strength. You offered me friendship. And that has made all the difference in the world.

In other words, I love you, Eddie. I'll always think of you as my second brother. You saved me from myself.

Unfortunately, nothing can save me now—except knowing that you and Sara will go on living. Be good to her, Eddie. She's hard on herself, and she needs your love. Take care of her. Help her forget the past and embrace the future.

And have a good life.

My eternal love,
Jessie

Folding the notes carefully, she stood up and looked around her bedroom. She'd lived in this room, this house, from the day she was born. It was filled with so many memories—and so many ghosts . . .

She could almost hear Josh upstairs, laughing and strumming his guitar, singing a love song he had written for Sara. Jessie tilted her head and listened.

But it was only the wind.

Crossing the bedroom, she picked up an old rag doll from her childhood. It was her favorite toy. It made her feel happy and safe. Hugging it and smelling it made her feel like a little girl without a care in the world. Suddenly it was Christmas, and Grandfather Frank was handing out gifts around the tree. Josh got a guitar, and Jessie got a doll. Everyone was laughing. Everyone was happy.

If only Christmas could last forever.

With tears in her eyes, Jessie stepped out of her bedroom and into the hall. She walked past the rooms where her mother and father slept when Jessie was just a baby. She was too young to remember them, but the sight of the locked bedroom door always made her feel warm—and loved.

"Good night, Mommy. Good night, Daddy," she whispered in a little girl voice, the same way she did when she said her prayers as a child, saying good night to her mommy and daddy in heaven.

Then she climbed the stairs, up to the fourth floor of the mansion—to Josh's room.

Her heart skipped a beat when she stepped inside. There were so many memories of Josh here—the posters on the walls, the clothes in the closet, the sheet music on the desk—all the pieces of a life cut short.

"Josh."

She whispered his name and pictured him sitting in the tower window with his guitar, looking out at the lake as he composed another song.

For the first time, Jessie realized that she was feeling the same pain that her brother felt before he killed himself—pain that he hid from his family and friends.

He, too, had been turning into a monster. He, too, knew the only way to escape.

Jessie's eyes filled with tears. Then, clutching the suicide notes in her hand, she walked across the room and opened the tower window.

The stone path below looked hard and cruel. She closed her eyes and tried to imagine jumping and falling, plunging down closer and closer to the path—closer to death.

Then she tried to imagine what Josh must have been thinking when he jumped. It was easy to do. Jessie was sure he was thinking the same things she was thinking right now . . .

About the people they loved.

And how much they'd miss them.

If only there was another way, Jessie thought. Then she looked down at the gray patches of rotted flesh on her arms—and she knew it was only a matter of time.

She closed her eyes and thought about Josh, Sara, Eddie, Baskerville—even Grandfather Frank. She loved them all so much, her heart began to ache. Because love was stronger than anything. Love would outlive all the fear, hate—and monsters—in the world.

But love couldn't save her now. Only death could.

Grasping the window frame with both hands and leaning forward, Jessie whispered a silent prayer. Her tears were flowing freely now, streaking her face and blurring her vision. A rush of madness swirled through her brain, urging her to lash out at the world, but she pushed the violent thoughts away, clinging to the love she felt in her heart for Sara, Eddie, and Josh.

Then, placing her knee on the wooden sill, Jessie swallowed her tears, took a deep breath . . .

And climbed out the window.

17

Blood Sisters

From the diary of Sara Watkins . . .

They say that a person's eyes are the windows of the soul. I have every reason to believe it's true.

The last time I saw Jessie, I knew something was wrong. We exchanged glances in the cemetery—just one quick look—before the police sirens sent us all scattering in the morning light. And in that single fleeting instant, I knew Jessie had given up hope. In her eyes, I saw darkness, despair, and surrender. I saw her soul looking out, longing to escape . . .

I never felt more helpless in all my life. My best friend was going to kill herself . . .

And there was nothing I could do to stop her.

As soon as Sara and Eddie reached the Frank family mansion, they split up and searched the house. Eddie checked the library and basement, while Sara ran up the stairs to look in Jessie's bedroom.

Baskerville was sleeping on Jessie's bed. Sara stroked his ears and asked him, "Where's Jessie? Huh, boy? We gotta find Jessie!"

The big black hound yawned and stretched, then

jumped up and barked. "Find Jessie!" Sara repeated. In a flash, the dog was up and out of the room, dashing down the hall. Sara followed him up the stairs, taking two at a time. Her pulse was racing.

Somehow, in her heart, she knew she didn't have a moment to lose.

She remembered the look in Jessie's eyes as her monstrous parents reached out for her in the cemetery. It looked as if Jessie was ready to give up—and join them.

Sara felt the tears burning her eyes as she reached the top of the stairs. Baskerville was running down the hall to Josh's bedroom. And that's when Sara knew she was probably too late.

Jessie had gone up to the highest tower of the mansion, where her brother committed suicide. She was going to follow in her brother's footsteps.

Don't do it, Jessie, Sara thought. Please don't do it. I can't lose you, too. I can't . . .

By the time she reached the bedroom door, Sara's heart was about to explode. Hot, salty tears scalded her face. But even expecting the worse, she was not prepared for what she saw when she flung open the door of Josh's room . . .

Jessie was climbing out of the window.

No, Jessie! No!

Something snapped inside of Sara—a silent scream that could find no voice. She was speechless, frozen with shock. But her heart was still strong, and it told her what to do.

Sara bolted across the room, diving at the window with upraised arms. She saw Jessie slowly disappear over the wooden sill. First, her head and torso, then her legs slipped away, falling, falling . . .

Sara unleashed a soul-shattering scream.

"*Jessie!!*"

She lunged forward . . .

And grabbed Jessie by the ankles.

Jessie's body struck the side of the house with a heavy thud. But she didn't fall. She dangled in the air like a puppet, suspended by strings of love, passion, and fury . . .

Sara screamed for strength, fueled by emotions. She tightened her grasp on Jessie's ankles and pulled with all her might.

I'm going to drop her, she thought in terror. I'm not strong enough to hold her . . .

And sure enough, with that one trace of doubt, Jessie began to slowly slip away, her ankles sliding out of Sara's grip.

"*Nooo!!*"

Sara screamed and pulled harder, blinded by tears of rage. Jessie was going to fall. Sara could feel her slipping away, inch by inch. Jessie was going to die— just like Josh . . .

There, in the highest tower of the mansion, the last of the Frankensteins would cross the threshold between life and death.

And once again, Sara was helpless to stop it.

Jessie slipped another inch out of her grasp. Sara cried out in shock and despair. It was all over now. She felt it in her heart. Jessie was falling, falling . . .

Until Eddie grabbed her by the legs.

He crowded into the window next to Sara, reaching out and pulling Jessie's legs with every bit of strength he had. Sara sobbed and tightened her grip, then helped Eddie pull, pull, pull the girl up and through the window . . .

Until Jessie spilled onto the floor at their feet, crying like a baby, hiding her face in shame.

Sara and Eddie leaned back against the window frame, gasping for air. They looked down at their friend, hardly able to move or speak. Finally Jessie managed to say something, her words broken by her sobs . . .

"Why? Why didn't you let me die? Why . . . ?"

Sara threw herself down, taking Jessie into her arms and crying uncontrollably. "Because we love you, you stupid jerk," she whispered. "I don't care if you do turn into a monster! We'll love you anyway, Jessie. We'll take you to doctors, we'll take care of you . . . anything. Just don't kill yourself, okay? Okay?"

Slowly Jessie looked up at Sara and Eddie. Her face was wet with tears, her eyes dark and haunted. "You two are such a pain," she muttered. "I even wrote you mushy suicide notes, and then you go and save my life. What a waste of time." She pulled the notes out of her robe and threw them on the floor.

Eddie smiled sadly. "It's the thought that counts," he said. "Anyway, if you hadn't wasted the time writing those notes, you'd be dead. And I, for one, am glad you're alive."

Jessie smirked bitterly. "You're glad *now*," she said. "But what about a few months from now . . . when I'm as rotted as a zombie?!!"

Sara pulled Jessie closer and whispered in her ear.

"You know if there's anything I can do . . . anything at all . . . I'll do it. For you."

The pool of tears in Jessie's eyes reflected all the love and fear in Sara's heart. "I know you would, Sara," she said. "But sometimes there's nothing you can do. It's not like the movies, you know. You can't expect a miracle cure and a happy ending."

The two girls hugged and wept in silence.

Eddie leaned back against the window frame and scratched his head. "You know, that reminds me of a movie I saw last night," he said. Sara and Jessie looked up at him as if he were crazy. "I know it sounds stupid, but I couldn't sleep so I watched this vampire movie on TV. They turned these vampires into mortals by giving them a blood transfusion. They drained out the vampire blood and replaced it with human blood."

Jessie rolled her eyes. "You're right, it's stupid."

But Sara stared down at the floor and bit her lip, lost in thought. "It could work," she said.

Jessie did a double take. "Are you kidding, Sara? It's a dumb special effect from a cheesy vampire movie!"

Sara shrugged. "Maybe so, but I think it could work!" She clenched her hand into a fist. "The monster strain is in your blood. Change the blood, delete the strain."

Jessie shook her head. "But where are we going to get that much blood?"

"You're looking at her," said Sara. "I have a whole body full of blood. You and I have the same blood type. Don't you remember?"

Jessie nodded, then looked up with a glimmer of hope in her eyes. "Do you really think it could work?"

Sara raised her hands in the air. "Jessie, really. What do we have to lose? Except a little time . . ."

"And a lot of blood," said Jessie.

Grandfather Frank's library was a room filled floor to ceiling with medical textbooks—and fully stocked with medical supplies. The velvet curtains were pulled shut over the tall windows, blocking out the noonday sun, and the rich dusty aroma of forbidden knowledge clawed at the air like a heady perfume.

Sara and Jessie lay side by side on two long, leather-upholstered benches, their sleeves rolled up and arms exposed.

Eddie had to help Sara with the needles and tubes. In the past, he would have been too squeamish to do it, but after resurrecting Josh, he could stomach just about anything. Sticking a needle into an arm was nothing compared to sewing severed limbs on a torso.

The tubes were connected to huge jars on the floor—jars that were now halfway full of blood. And as the blood flowed from the two girls' arms into the jars, Eddie could see the color draining from their faces.

"You two look so pale," he said. "Are you sure that's not enough? I don't want to bleed you dry."

Sara slowly lifted her head and glanced down at the thick red liquid in the jars. "More," she whispered.

She felt so weak and dizzy, as if she were going to pass out. She could feel her own life force draining away, drop by drop. It was more than a little frightening.

Then she turned her head and looked at Jessie. Jessie stared back with eyes brimming with tears. There was such warmth there, such love, it washed away any fears Sara had.

"Okay, Eddie," she whispered. "Take my blood and feed it into Jessie."

Eddie removed the needle from Sara's arm, then picked up the jar of blood and placed it on Grandfather Frank's desk. Then he hooked it up to another needle and found an artery under Jessie's skin. Soon, Sara's blood was flowing freely from the jar, through the tube—into Jessie's body.

"Do you think that'll do it?" said Eddie.

Sara looked up, her face white. "We may have to do it a few more times," she answered in a daze. "Whatever it takes. Even if we have to stay here all day. There's more blood where that came from . . ."

Her voice trailed off, and her head fell to the side. She blinked and gazed at Jessie, who didn't take her eyes off her. Jessie smiled through her tears.

"You know, Sara," she whispered. "We're really sisters now, you and I. Blood sisters."

She reached out for Sara's hand.

A single tear rolled down Sara's cheek as she stretched out her hand for Jessie. Their fingers touched, their hands clasped together.

Jessie's words echoed in Sara's brain . . .

Sisters.

And she experienced a warm rush of love that went far beyond flesh and blood.

"I always wanted a sister, Jessie," she whispered. "I think you're the best."

Jessie glanced up at Eddie, then looked back at Sara. She could feel her own heart beating, the warm fresh blood flowing through her veins and arteries.

"You're the only family I have now." Jessie closed her eyes and wept. She felt the pain in her heart. Then she opened her eyes again. "I love you guys."

Sara couldn't stop herself from crying. She felt so weak from the loss of blood, her emotions had risen to the surface. She couldn't hide her feelings any longer.

"I love you, Jessie," she whispered. "And I love you, Eddie. Love you . . . both of you . . . forever . . ."

Then she faded off, closing her eyes and drifting away like a ship on the open seas, rolling with the waves. Jessie, too, nodded off in a dreamy haze.

After a few minutes, Eddie removed the needles, repositioning the jars and repeating the entire process. Occasionally one of the girls would look up and mumble, "I love you," then drift off to dreamland again.

The transfusion was completed in several hours. The blood of Frankenstein was replaced with the blood of mortals. Sara and Jessie were peaceful now . . .

The curse was lifted.

As the girls lay resting on the upholstered benches, Eddie scanned the books in Grandfather Frank's library Every branch of science was represented here, in volume after volume of chemistry, biology, mathematics, even nuclear physics. He had never seen such a complete collection. It was mind-boggling.

He reached up for an unusual series of medical books from the Orient. Their spines were so beautiful, he wanted to take a closer look.

But when he tried to take one off the shelf, the whole row of spines dropped down on a hinge . . .

It was a secret hiding place.

And it was full of dusty old journals.

Eddie grabbed two of the leather-bound notebooks and opened one up. It was handwritten in pen and ink, the curving letters faded with time.

He recognized the handwriting.

It belonged to Victor Frankenstein, the man who created a monster over two hundred years ago. Eddie remembered his curvy lettering from the original journal they'd used to resurrect Josh.

But there was something odd about this journal.

It was dated 1883.

That's impossible, Eddie thought to himself. Victor Frankenstein must have died in the early 1800s.

Reaching up for another journal, Eddie flipped through and saw the same handwriting—but this time it was dated 1910!

What's going on here? he wondered.

The only thing to do was to take them all down and read them. Which was exactly what Eddie did. He sat down in an overstuffed chair with the entire stack of journals and started reading. It was quite a task, and it took him several hours.

But by the time Sara and Jessie woke up, Eddie had quite a story to tell them . . .

The true story of Frankenstein.

‡•‡

18

Frankenstein the Victor

From the secret journal of Professor Frank . . .

Sara, Jessie, and Eddie have survived last night's attack. I don't know how, but it's true.

Now they are armed with knowledge. They have seen my creations, old and new, and they know what they're up against. They probably know that I am still alive, resurrected after death. Perhaps they have discovered the hidden journals in my library—and know the truth of my existence.

Knowledge is power.

But knowledge will not save Sara, Jessie, and Eddie. In the war between the living and the dead, only the strong will survive—and death will be the victor . . .

Because you can't kill what is already dead.

Sara opened her eyes and stared at the ceiling of the library. She blinked twice, confused by her surroundings, then remembered where she was—and what had happened.

"Wake up, sleepyhead," someone whispered.

Sara turned her head. Jessie and Eddie were sitting at the desk with a tray of sandwiches and grape juice.

Jessie winked at her and smiled. "You were snoring," she said.

"No way," Sara mumbled, sitting up slowly and rubbing her eyes. She yawned and then glanced at the velvet drapes on the windows. Not a trace of light peeped through; it was dark outside. "I feel like I've been sleeping for weeks. What time is it?" she asked.

Eddie looked at his watch. "Almost eight o'clock. How do you feel?"

Sara sat upright and stretched. "A little weak, but okay."

"You need to eat something," said Eddie, handing her a sandwich and a glass of juice. "Grape juice is good for your blood. I read that somewhere."

Sara took a bite of the sandwich, then a sip of the juice. "Not bad." She felt better almost immediately. Her body craved nourishment.

Jessie and Eddie watched her eat in silence. With each bite, Sara felt her body growing stronger—and her mind growing clearer.

"Feel better?" asked Jessie.

Sara swallowed. "Who cares about me? What about you, Jessie? How do *you* feel?"

The dark-haired girl stared back at her with a blank, somber expression. Then, slowly, a tiny smile crept over Jessie's face.

"I feel *great!*" she cried out, hardly able to contain herself. "I feel strong and healthy . . . and *normal*. I feel *human* again, Sara. Thanks to you . . ."

Tears welled up in Jessie's eyes. She jumped up from her chair and hugged Sara as hard as she could.

"Thanks to *both* of you," she gasped, reaching out for Eddie, "I feel like myself again."

Eddie crossed the room, throwing his arms around the two crying girls—and crying just as hard as either one of them. A powerful wave of emotion swept through them all, binding their hearts and souls together for all eternity.

Never again would they have friends they loved so truly, so closely, so passionately . . .

Friends for life. Friends to the end. Friends everlasting.

They held each other for a long time, weeping gently in the darkness of the library. Finally Jessie pulled away and wiped the tears from her eyes.

"You have to tell her, Eddie," she said. "Tell Sara what you started to tell me."

Eddie stood up and cleared his throat. His eyes were red and wet, but he wasn't ashamed. Not in front of his closest friends. "See that?" he said, pointing to the stack of dusty journals on the floor.

Sara leaned forward and nodded.

"They're the journals of Victor Frankenstein," he said. "And they explain how Grandfather Frank came back from the dead."

A puzzled look crossed Sara's face. How could the journals of the man who created a monster two hundred years ago explain the modern-day resurrection of Grandfather Frank? "What are you talking about?" she asked.

Eddie picked up a journal and sat down. "It's simple. Grandfather Frank is not who or what you think he is. He's hardly human at all . . . He's a collection of body parts sewn together."

Sara's mouth dropped open. "You mean, Grand-father Frank is just another monster created by Victor Frankenstein?"

"No," said Eddie, leaning back in his chair. "Grand-father Frank *is* Victor Frankenstein."

After the shock of Eddie's words sunk in, Sara and Jessie started assaulting him with question after question. Finally Eddie told them to shut up and listen . . .

"These journals," he said, pointing, "begin in 1799 and continue through the years to the present. And they're all written by Victor Frankenstein. Look, you can see. It's all in the same handwriting."

He handed a couple journals to Sara and Jessie. They flipped through them and nodded. "But how?" asked Jessie.

"Well," said Eddie, "Victor Frankenstein didn't die in the frozen wastelands, like in the book by Mary Shelley. He *did* chase the monster there, but he caught it . . . and chopped off its head."

"I know. I've seen it," said Jessie, remembering the gruesome head stitched on the dog's body.

Eddie continued. "Frankenstein returned to Europe with the head in a bag and set up a new laboratory in Waterloo, where Napoleon's bloody defeat in 1815 supplied the mad doctor with hundreds of corpses. There, he carried on his work in secret."

Sara shook her head. "I don't know whether to call him a dedicated scientist . . . or a ghoul."

Eddie frowned. "It gets worse," he said. "In 1830, another revolution in France sparked revolts throughout Europe, in Belgium, Poland, Germany . . . wherever the tide of death flowed, Victor Frankenstein was there to pick up the pieces."

"Yuck," said Jessie.

Sara sighed. "But wasn't it dangerous? Wasn't he getting too old?"

"That's the funny thing," said Eddie. "It *was* dangerous, and he *was* getting old. One day, he received a bullet wound in the leg. He passed out from pain, and when he woke up, he discovered that a surgeon had removed his leg to stop the infection. For Frankenstein, it was a stroke of luck. Because he found out that he could replace his *own* body parts . . . using the same techniques that spawned his creatures."

Sara and Jessie gasped.

"You can imagine what he did next," said Eddie. "Bit by bit, he replaced every limb and organ in his body. He even blackmailed other doctors to help him transplant his own heart . . . and transfer his own brain into another head."

The room was silent. Terrible, grisly images flashed through Sara's and Jessie's minds.

"What did he do then?" Sara asked. "He achieved immortality. What more could he want?"

Eddie's face turned grim. "He wanted to create a race of superhumans, perfect in every way. But the results of his experiments were always monstrous. His creatures had no souls, though Frankenstein denied the existence of the soul. He refused to give up. He roamed the far corners of the world, ravaging the human remains of the bloodiest wars. Like the Opium War in China, the Mexican War, the Civil War, the Russian Revolutions, World War I and II . . . Where there was death, there was Frankenstein."

Sara's head was spinning. It was impossible for her mind to grasp the sheer volume of carnage—and the tragic cycle of life and death.

"You've heard of Jack the Ripper?" said Eddie. "Scotland Yard suspected the killer was a surgeon. And they were right. It was Victor Frankenstein . . ."

Jessie shook her head in disbelief. "You mean, *Grandfather Frank?*"

Like a bolt of lightning, the name struck immediate terror in the hearts of the three teenagers. The horrors of the past disappeared—and the nightmare of the present came rushing in, jolting them back to reality.

Sara glanced at the windows. "We shouldn't be here," she said. "It's dark outside. He'll be sending those monsters after us."

Jessie began to tremble. "Where should we go?"

Sara took a deep breath. "The last place he'll ever think of looking for us."

"And where's that?" asked Eddie.

Sara smiled.

"The old mill," she said.

The moon sank lower in the horizon, until the black waters of Thunder Lake swallowed it whole. Still, under a shroud of darkness, the ever-turning waterwheel and pointed roof of the mill stood out against the night sky.

Because the darkness within was even blacker.

Sara, Jessie, and Eddie crept along the side of the old wooden structure, their hearts beating faster than the grinding gears of the wheel. They moved silently toward the lowest end of the roof, then climbed up, one by one, crawling on their hands and knees to the small tower on top. The sounds of their footsteps were masked by the churning water and endless grind of the wheel.

When they reached the rooftop, they crouched around the tower and peered down through the broken windows—at the laboratory below . . .

There was a body on the table.

A new monster.

And Grandfather Frank was hunched over it, adjusting the bolts in its neck.

Even after last night's attack, Sara, Eddie, and Jessie had never seen anything quite as horrifying—or grotesque—as the thing on the lab table. It was like a jigsaw puzzle constructed from the scattered pieces of a dozen different puzzles. Nothing matched, nothing fit, nothing made sense . . .

Its head was that of an old woman, but its torso belonged to a muscular man. One arm was thin and wiry and the color of cocoa. The other was thick and flabby and whiter than snow. The hips were wide and shapely, like a beauty queen past her prime. One hand was hairy with sausagelike fingers; the other, slender with pink painted nails. The legs were knock-kneed—but at least they were a matched set.

Grandfather Frank made a final adjustment and stepped back. "Arise, my child!" he screamed.

The jigsaw creature didn't move.

"Arise, I said! Get up and walk! You're alive, my child! You're not beautiful . . . but you're alive! Get up!"

Sara, Jessie, and Eddie thought Grandfather Frank had finally cracked. The thing on the table was the sloppiest work he'd ever done. The stitches were loose and torn. The steel clamps were barely attached. And there was no way in heaven or hell that trash heap could possibly be alive.

But Thunder Lake was neither heaven nor hell . . .

So it shouldn't have been such a surprise when the sausagelike fingers started to twitch.

The thin arm throbbed while the flabby arm flapped. The old lady's lips puckered, and the torso flexed. Then, with its knobby white knees knocking together, the jigsaw creature sat up on the table . . .

And screamed.

"Yes! Yes!" howled Grandfather Frank, his head bobbing back and forth on his broken neck. "Arise, my child! Arise!"

The mix-and-match monster flopped its legs over the side of the lab table, standing up slowly with a twitch and a jerk. Then, like a misfit toy, it took two steps forward . . .

And fell to pieces.

Jessie covered her eyes, but Sara and Eddie were too stunned and horrified to look away. The scattered pieces of the monster wriggled and squirmed across the floor as Grandfather Frank roared with anger.

"No! No! No! Everything's ruined! Ruined!"

Suddenly he stopped and leaned against the lab table. Then he laughed like a demented fiend.

"Who needs you, anyway?! I have *more* than enough creatures to do my work! *More* than enough to kill Jessie and Sara and Eddie . . . and *more* than enough to resurrect them as Frankenstein's children! They're mine! Mine! Mine!"

The three teenagers on the roof trembled with fear.

"I'll get them . . . one by one . . . even if I have to do it *myself*!" He kicked the old woman's head across the room and screamed with laughter. Then he crawled on top of the lab table . . .

And fell asleep.

The teenagers didn't dare move or speak—until they heard the sounds of his snores up in the tower . . .

"What are we going to do?" Jessie whispered. "Where are we going to go?"

"I say we stay right here," said Sara.

"Here?" said Eddie, glancing nervously down at the grisly scene in the laboratory below.

"The monsters are out looking for us now," Sara explained. "We can't go home until daylight . . . when the monsters return."

Eddie sighed.

Jessie rolled over on her back and stared up at the sky. "He's totally insane," she whispered. "A complete psychopath. It's hard to believe that I lived my whole life thinking he's my grandfather." A tear trickled down Jessie's face. "I loved him, you know."

Sara reached out for Jessie's hand. "Me, too," she whispered. "He was a great man. A brilliant scientist.

And a pretty wonderful grandfather. Remember him
the way he used to be, Jessie. That man down there
is not Grandfather Frank. The fall damaged his brain.
He's not the same person."

Jessie sighed and wiped her tears. For a long time,
no one said a word. They lay on their backs and stared
up at the darkness. Jessie thought about her grandfather, and remembered how he'd give her piggyback
rides up and down the stairs when she was little. Sara
thought about Josh, and how much she loved him and
how much she missed him. Where was he now? Was
he thinking of her, too? And Eddie was wondering
how this big horrible mess was going to end.

Then, after a few minutes of silence, Jessie sat up
and whispered, "This is a stupid thing to bring up
now . . . but what about the Homecoming Game and
the dance? It's tomorrow night."

"You're right," said Eddie with a smirk. "Homecoming *does* sound stupid after all this."

Sara propped herself up on her elbows. "Wait a
minute," she said. "Maybe it's not so stupid."

Eddie and Jessie looked at her blankly.

"Think about it," Sara explained. "If we go to the
Homecoming Game tomorrow night, we'll be surrounded by hundreds of people. Everyone will be
looking at us. We'll be perfectly safe . . . at least for
a while. It gives us time to come up with a plan."

Eddie and Jessie considered the possibilities.

"And besides," said Sara, "I already bought a new
dress."

19

The Homecoming

From the high school newspaper, *The Weekly Thunder . . .*

VICTORY OR DEFEAT??

Forget about monsters. Forget about grave robbers. Tonight is the game to end all games—our final bid for the championship trophy in the toughest gridiron season ever. In tonight's Homecoming Football Game, the Thunder Lake Thunderbolts take on our fiercest arch-rivals, the Blue Mountain Eagles. Thunder Lake team captain, Crusher Surmacz, is confident that victory will be ours.

"We're gonna kill 'em," said Crusher in an exclusive interview. "We're gonna tear 'em limb from limb, then rip off their heads and eat their hearts."

Pregame activities begin at 7:00 P.M., and include the Victory Bonfire, the Homecoming Pep Rally, and the Crowning of This Year's Homecoming Queen. Kickoff at 7:30 P.M. And don't miss the big Homecoming Dance after the game!

Go, Thunderbolts, go!!

Every living soul in the town of Thunder Lake, Pennsylvania, felt the tension in the air.

It began with the setting of the sun. Storekeepers closed their shops early, the colorful school banners waving proudly in their windows. Parents checked to make sure they had film in their cameras, then loaded their cars with blankets and containers of hot coffee. Students and teachers surrounded the stadium, pushing and buzzing through the entrance gates like bees coming home to the hive.

It was Homecoming Night. A night of victory—or defeat. And everyone was hungry for blood.

The football players were hungry. The cheerleaders were hungry. Even the mommies and daddies who crowded into the bleachers were hungry for blood.

They licked their lips and cheered as a huge truckload of wood was piled up at the end of the field beyond the goalposts. Broken furniture, tree branches, planks and boards were tossed on the heap, and the towering stack rose higher and higher—until it was nearly fifteen feet high.

Then someone struck a match . . .

And the night exploded into flame.

"Strike-'em-dead, Thun-der-bolts! Strike-'em-dead, Thun-der-bolts!"

The cheerleaders danced around the roaring fire like natives of the jungle, chanting and shrieking, kicking and clapping. The flames grew brighter and stronger, the white-hot tongues lashing upward, blazing in the darkness.

"Strike-'em-dead, Thun-der-bolts!"

The crowd roared . . .

And the cheerleaders lifted a human sacrifice into the air.

It was a stuffed scarecrow, wearing the uniform of their enemy. The chanting girls carried it over their heads, passing it around the circle of fire as the football players watched on and hissed.

The crowd cried out for blood.

The scarecrow soared through the air . . .

And plunged downward into the flames. The uniform caught fire almost instantly. Then the raggedy arms and legs started to burn. Soon the whole body was blistering and blazing like a hideous human torch.

And a chant rose up from every man, woman, and child in Thunder Lake. A steady, rhythmic chorus of voices that grew stronger and stronger, then faster and faster . . .

"Kill! Kill! *Kill! Kill! KILL! KILL! KILL!*"

The creature watched with fear in his eyes.

He stood in the shadows of the school, looking down at the horrifying scene in the stadium—the crowd, the fire, the killing . . .

And he wondered why people had to be so cruel.

Maybe the man they killed was ugly, too. Like he was. Maybe they would kill *all* things that were ugly, and different, and alone.

The thing that used to be Josh didn't want to die that way—by fire. Fire brought pain. Terrible pain. So he stepped deeper into the shadows and crawled along the edge of the school, hiding from those who killed with fire.

He sat, trembling and cold, thrusting his hands into his pockets. His huge fingers touched the tiny gold ring. He stroked it and held it tightly in his hand . . .

Sara.

He thought about the girl with yellow hair. So sweet. So pretty. And he remembered the feelings she stirred in his heart . . .

Love.

He looked out at the burning flames, and wondered if they really hurt more than the pain in his heart—the agony of a love that never died. Love was the reason he came here, searching for Sara. He needed to protect her.

The dead wanted to kill her.

But now he was afraid. Of the angry people. And the roaring flames.

His cold green eyes glowed in the darkness—and glistened with tears. Because he understood that love was more powerful than death. And he knew what he had to do, in spite of his fear . . .

He had to go down there among the people and flames.

He had to help Sara.

Peering through the bushes, the creature waited until a small group of teenagers walked by—then he darted across the path toward the stadium gates. He staggered along the fence, moving closer to the blazing bonfire, and ducked into another cluster of bushes. The creature crouched down, his oversized body hidden by leaves. Then he pressed his gray, scarred face against the chain link fence—and looked in . . .

The girls were dancing and singing around the fire.

They looked so pretty in the orange light, almost as pretty as Sara.

The creature's eyes locked on the face of a small girl with short dark hair. He knew this girl. And he loved her in a different way than he loved Sara. Long ago, when he was still alive, the dark-haired girl was someone special . . .

Sister.

The word echoed in the creature's brain—and amplified the loneliness in his soul. His face was streaked with tears as he watched his sister Jessie from afar.

Then the creature looked over at a small stage near the bonfire. There were people standing on the platform, boys and girls wearing bright and pretty clothes.

The creature gasped . . .

Because Sara was there on the stage with them.

Sara.

She looked so beautiful, so radiant—the creature's heart began to ache just looking at her. The memory of her words whispered in his head . . .

I love you, Josh. Forever.

The creature sighed with longing as he grasped the chain link fence in his powerful fingers. His love intensified his anguish. His passion fueled his tears . . .

And his hands tore a hole in the fence.

Sara sat down next to Eddie in one of the folding chairs on stage—and waited nervously for the Big Moment.

Any minute now, a booming voice on the loudspeaker would announce the name of This Year's Homecoming Queen . . .

And Sara would find out if her nightmare was going to come true.

She glanced at the glittering crown on the podium. It certainly didn't *look* like the crown in her dream—a sharp and deadly headpiece made from scalpels. The real crown was beautiful. But that didn't make Sara feel any better . . .

The real nightmares were *out there*, in the darkness outside the stadium.

"Do you suppose they're watching us?" she whispered to Eddie. "Right now?"

Eddie straightened his tie and looked out over the heads of the crowd. "I doubt it," he said. "Not with all these people here. And that bonfire. Look at that thing burn! You can feel the heat from here!"

Sara stared into the blaze, mesmerized by the dancing flames. There was something hypnotic, even haunting, about it—something deeply disturbing. On the night that Josh killed himself, she dreamed about fire. Now, staring into the flames, she realized it was a force of nature every bit as powerful and mysterious as lightning and thunder.

"Jessie's a great little cheerleader," said Eddie, breaking her thoughts. "Look at her go!"

Sara focused her eyes on her best friend. Jessie looked so cute, bouncing up and down and moving to the rhythm. Her face was glowing, radiant. She looked vibrant, healthy—and alive.

"She's beautiful," Sara muttered softly.

Eddie reached out for Sara's hand and squeezed

it. "*You're* beautiful," he said, suddenly filled with emotion.

Sara turned and looked at Eddie, touched by the sincerity in his voice, his eyes . . .

"You're not just beautiful on the outside," he said. "You're beautiful *here*, too." He touched his heart and tried to smile. But his face betrayed his truer, deeper feelings. "Everything you did for Josh, for Jessie . . . and for me . . . it came from the heart, Sara."

She squeezed his hand and blinked back her tears. She knew what he was trying to say to her—the same words echoed in her mind and pierced her heart every time she looked at Eddie Perez . . .

"I love you, Sara," he said.

Sara's lip trembled.

"I want you to run away with me," he whispered with quiet intensity. "We can leave this town . . . tonight . . . run away and never look back again."

Her vision blurred with tears. She tried to imagine saying good-bye to all her memories—all the places and things that made up her life. Her house, her family, her memories of Josh—her first true love. She stared at the bonfire and sighed. "What about Jessie? She has no family anymore."

Eddie didn't hesitate. "We'll bring her with us."

Then Sara turned her head and stared out at the darkness beyond the stadium. "What about *them*?" she asked. "What about Grandfather Frank and his monsters?"

Eddie cleared his throat. "We'll go to another town and make an anonymous phone call to the police. We'll tell them where the grave robbers are hiding.

And we'll warn them how dangerous they are."

Sara couldn't speak. Her mind was racing, her heart breaking in two. Running away seemed too simple, too easy—like suicide. Yes, it was possible to save yourself, to end the pain forever. But you couldn't help hurting the people you loved most of all . . .

Her voice cracked when she tried to speak. "And what about . . . what about Josh?"

Eddie lowered his head and stared down at the stage floor. He didn't have an answer for her question. Every time he thought about Josh—and pictured the sadness reflected in Josh's cold green eyes—Eddie felt a twinge of pain. He recognized that look. It came from the bottom of the soul, a sense of despair he had felt himself so many times . . .

It was loneliness. Frustration. Longing.

No matter what happened tonight, someone was going to get hurt. Eddie knew that for a fact, but couldn't do anything about it.

Suddenly a voice rang out from the loudspeakers: *"And now, ladies and gentlemen, we'd like to introduce our Homecoming candidates one last time! Remember, only one special girl can become Thunder Lake's Homecoming Queen! And here are this year's couples!!"*

Sara and Eddie each took a deep breath. Their hearts were pounding in their chests as they stood up and stepped forward. A spotlight glared in their eyes. The crowd whistled and cheered . . .

The Big Moment had arrived.

Beyond the circle of fire and light, there was darkness. And within the darkness, there were eyes . . .

Watching. Waiting.

In the shadows of the school, the gray rotted corpses of a mother and father shambled toward the light, their bony hands stretched out, searching for their children.

On the path near the stadium gates, the resurrected bodies of two teenage boys stared at the passing crowd with hungry dead eyes.

By the chain link fence, a murdered cheerleader with electric hair stalked the night like a cat after a mouse.

And down beneath the bleachers, a living nightmare with a human head and a dog's body sniffed through the garbage—scavenging for blood.

Suddenly, the sound of cheers and the flashing of light pulled their attention toward the bonfire and stage. The creatures stumbled forward, hiding in the shadows as they scanned the crowd for their victims . . .

And that's when the eyes of the dead fell upon Sara, Eddie, and Jessie.

"And This Year's Homecoming Queen is . . ."

The crowd held their breath and waited.

" . . . Sara Watkins!!!"

A huge roar rose up from the students and parents and fans. Cameras flashed, hands clapped, and confetti showered the stage. Then Principal Frear stepped forward with a giant bouquet of roses, placing them in the arms of a young teenage girl who looked too shocked for words.

"Let's hear it for Sara Watkins . . . Thunder Lake's Homecoming Queen!"

Music filled the air as Sara stepped forward, blinking back her tears and squinting against the glare of the light. She hugged the roses and smiled nervously, then leaned forward as the master of ceremonies placed the glittering crown on her head.

It all seemed so unreal—a dazzling fantasy world, light-years away from the pain and darkness of death and resurrection that had taken over her life. After all the tragedy she'd seen, Sara had forgotten the simple joys and rituals of the real world, the power of a smile, the beauty of roses . . .

For a brief instant, she closed her eyes and pictured the faces of the people she loved. Jessie . . . smiling and cracking jokes. Eddie . . . sweet, goofy, and filled with affection. Josh . . . loving and passionate— and *alive*.

When Sara opened her eyes, they were filled with tears. She looked out at the crowd, saw the pride on her parents' faces, the joy in her grandparents' smiles. Then she turned and reached out her hand for Eddie.

Eddie . . .

My love.

He stepped forward, handsome and beaming as he took her into his arms and kissed her—passionately, tenderly, not caring at all if the whole world looked on, kissing her like a lover, not a friend.

And for one glorious moment, Sara forgot everything about the nightmare that haunted her soul—the

suicide of her boyfriend, the curse that brought him
back, and the monsters who rose up to stalk them.

Every horrible tragedy faded from her mind, like a
long-forgotten dream . . .

Until someone started screaming.

Sara's thoughts were shattered in a second as the
screaming rang out near the gates of the stadium. Her
heart almost stopped when the screams multiplied and
grew. And her worst nightmare came true as the terror
swept through the crowd like a virus . . .

And the monsters attacked.

20

The Mob

From the diary of Sara Watkins . . .

When I heard the first scream, I knew that all hell was about to break loose.

But it was even worse than I ever imagined.

On this fateful night in November, a Homecoming football game became a very different kind of blood sport. Terror turned into rage, and rage turned into violence. Every dark impulse buried in the soul came rising up, screaming, like a monster from the grave.

I'm not even talking about the living dead. I'm referring to ordinary people like you and me, your parents and your teachers. Inside every one of us, there is a monster . . .

And tonight, we saw the mirror image of our souls.

Jessie Frank was having the time of her life—before the screaming started . . .

Cheering with her classmates around the roaring bonfire, jumping up and down, dancing and clapping, she'd never felt so alive. Her mind was clear, her body strong. And in spite of the horrors that cursed her family, she had to admit she was having fun. Even her skin was clearing up. She could feel the gray patches of rotting death flake away beneath her cheerleader's uniform. It was a little uncomfortable, but so what? She was alive . . .

And all the boys were looking at her!

"Go, team, go!!"

She cheered as loud as she could and kicked her legs in the air. Who ever knew cheerleading could be such a hoot?

Then it was time to announce the Homecoming Queen. Jessie stood with the other cheerleaders and looked up at the stage, grinning from ear to ear.

Sara looked so beautiful. Eddie, too, in his suit and tie. They made such a cute couple, Jessie could hardly stand it. Her heart was bursting with pride—and love.

When the voice on the loudspeaker declared Sara Watkins the winner, no one screamed louder than Jessie . . .

Because no one knew the heartache and pain that tortured Sara as well as Jessie did.

Sara deserved the crown. She deserved all the love and happiness the world could offer. Jessie couldn't stop her tears from flowing as she watched Sara accept the roses in her arms and the crown on her head. It was like a dream come true—a shining ray of light at the end of the tunnel.

But Jessie was wrong about that. It wasn't the light at the end of the tunnel. It was the calm before the storm.

Of course, Jessie had no way of knowing that . . .

Until someone started screaming.

The piercing cry made her turn and look toward the gates of the stadium. Something was happening. People were screaming and running. Others were knocked down to the ground as two monstrous figures stomped through the crowd, growling and roaring and swinging their fists . . .

It was Moose and Mike Morgan.

And they were heading right for her.

Jessie spun around in a panic, glancing at the stage and seeing the look of shock on Sara's face. Then Jessie heard another burst of screams from the bleachers . . .

She turned to look.

It was the demonic dog-creature—and it was leaping across the stands, its hideous, monstrous head snapping at men, women, and children.

People crowded into the aisles, shrieking and pushing their way out, even if they had to step on others to do it. A riot broke out on the bleachers. Some teenagers jumped over the sides, falling to the ground with a sickening crunch. It was every man for himself.

Jessie turned her head back toward the gates . . .

The Morgan boys were closing in, punching and clawing every person who stood in their way. Everybody was screaming. They feared for their lives as the brain-dead brothers kicked them aside . . .

Jessie knew she had to get away. And fast.

She turned to run—and froze . . .

Her mother and father were standing in front of her.

Jessie screamed.

And her parents grabbed her. Their thin, bony

arms wrapped around her shoulders and pulled her close. She could smell the stench of the grave on their breath—as they lowered their heads and tried to kiss her.

"Noooo!"

Jessie had no idea if her dead mother and father wanted to save her or kill her—but she didn't want to find out. With a burst of superhuman strength, she shouted at the top of her lungs and broke away, falling onto the ground.

Her fellow cheerleaders shrieked like a chorus of police sirens. But nobody helped her. Not even the football players.

Jessie looked up in horror. Her parents loomed over her, moving closer and closer. Their flesh was almost completely rotted away. Their eyes flickered and burned—with hate? With love? Jessie wondered if she should wait and see what they'd do—but when they got close enough for her to see the worms burrowing into their flesh, her first impulse was to scream. Her second impulse was to run.

Jumping to her feet, Jessie dashed around the roaring bonfire . . .

Where she came face-to-face with Mike Morgan.

The dead freshman boy stared back at her with lifeless eyes. But then a spark of recognition twisted his face into a leering grin. He puckered his lips and started making kissing sounds. Then he reached out with his hands—and came after her.

Jessie screamed and plunged into the crowd of cheerleaders, who scattered in terror. Mike Morgan shoved them aside, stomping on their pom-poms as he growled and licked his yellow lips. Jessie collided with a mob of hysterical people. It was too crowded to push through, so she dropped to the ground and tried to crawl under their legs.

But Mike Morgan caught her by the ankle . . .

And dragged her away.

Sara and Eddie looked down from the stage—at the carnage below.

The entire stadium had erupted into a full-scale riot. Wherever they looked, there seemed to be a monster, biting and clawing its way through the crowds. In panic and fear, the people were as brutal as the monsters themselves, knocking each other down, pushing and trampling and screaming for their lives. The sound was almost deafening.

Sara watched in horror as Jessie was dragged through the crowds by the corpse of Mike Morgan. She pounded her fists against the ground and wailed. And her zombielike parents lunged after them.

"Jessie!!!!"

Sara shouted at the top of her lungs, but it was useless.

A screaming throng of people swarmed around the stage like a human tidal wave. Sara and Eddie stood helplessly, staring over the crowd, knowing there was nowhere to go, nowhere to run . . .

They were trapped.

Suddenly Sara noticed a blaze of sparks near the chain link fence. She looked over and saw Heather Leigh Clark clinging to the fence. Her hair bristled with electric light. Her eyes glowed with unearthly rage. And her bloodstained lips pulled back from her teeth as she hissed—at Sara.

"Eddie, look!"

Sara pointed toward the dead cheerleader, then gasped as Heather tore through the fence with her clawlike hands. Like a demon from hell, she darted past the bonfire. And like a monstrous cat, she leapt into the crowd.

People screamed in pain and terror as Heather Leigh Clark clawed her way over their heads, digging her nails into their faces, their shoulders, their arms . . .

But no one was more horrified than Sara. Because Sara knew she was coming for *her*.

"Stand behind me!" Eddie shouted. "I'll try to fight her off!"

But Eddie never got the chance . . .

Because the bloated corpse of Moose Morgan flopped up onto the stage like a great white shark, sinking his teeth into Eddie's ankle.

Eddie howled—and fell to his knees.

Then Heather pounced on top of Sara.

The creature couldn't stand it any longer.

The other dead ones were hurting the people he loved.

Sara.

They wanted her dead.

Like me.

Josh roared with rage. And burst through the fence like a wild beast uncaged.

He staggered through the crowd, ignoring the horrified cries that rang in his ears—and the bottles and cans that showered down upon him.

The people were fighting back now.

Josh was terrified. He knew the people would throw him in the fire if they had the chance. But he didn't care.

Sara was in trouble.

He pushed and shoved his way through the sea of people. He could see Sara and his yellow-haired bride fighting on the stage, thrashing back and forth, their hands around each other's necks. There were two boys on stage, too. One was dead, the other alive. Both were kicking and clawing and biting like animals.

Suddenly, Sara went down.

The she-creature jumped on top of her.

And the thing that used to be Josh opened his mouth and bellowed in helpless rage . . .

"SA . . . RA!!!"

Tears filled the creature's eyes—and a sudden agonizing pain tore into his left hand. He looked down and roared.

His hand was trapped in the jaws of a gruesome animal. An animal with a gray dead face like his own. A face with stitches and scars and glowing green eyes.

And this animal-thing was chewing his hand off!

Josh howled and swung his arm from side to side. But the beast wouldn't let go. Its black body and legs slammed against the people in the crowd, who shrieked and ducked for cover.

The monster-dog's teeth sunk deeper and deeper

into his wrist. Any moment now, he knew he'd lose his hand . . .

Suddenly, another animal attacked.

It was Baskerville, the dog who loved him when he was alive. Now the hound was a monster, too. Just like his master.

Growling and lunging, the black dog sank his fangs into the monster-dog's throat.

The hellish beast howled . . .

And let go of Josh's hand.

Josh staggered backward, gripping his torn wrist and heading for the stage. There were people everywhere, running and screaming. He shoved them aside as he stumbled forward, reaching up and grasping the edge of the stage.

They were gone.

No Sara. No bride. No boys fighting.

A desperate cry escaped Josh's lips as he turned and stared at the maddening scene in the stadium. His mother and father terrorized the crowd, their rotted arms swiping at the faces of shocked onlookers. Baskerville and the animal-thing were locked in a brutal dogfight, rolling across the ground, fighting tooth and claw. Jessie and Eddie thrashed and screamed as the Morgan boys carried them, like trophies, over the heads of the crowds who stampeded the exit gate. And forty feet away, on the other side of the chain link fence, Heather Leigh Clark hissed like a snake . . .

And pulled Sara through a hole in the fence.

Josh watched in stunned silence. A wave of total helplessness and despair overwhelmed his soul. Loneliness and pain seized his heart. And every hope and dream he'd ever had, every desperate plea for love and happiness, came bursting out of him in one terrible, gut-wrenching cry . . .

"SA . . . RAAAA!!!"

Like a wolf baying at the moon, the lonesome wail of a single siren rose up in the town of Thunder Lake. Soon, it was joined by another, then another, until the empty streets echoed with the loud, piercing shrieks of a siren choir.

In the stadium, the crowd was no longer a crowd.

Now the good people of Thunder Lake had become a mob.

And a mob is something to fear.

Jimbo and Crusher were the first to fight back. As Moose Morgan dragged Jessie away, the two high school football players picked up bottles from the ground . . .

And smashed them down over Moose's head.

If they recognized Moose as their former football captain, it didn't make a difference. They were ready for a fight. And fight they did.

But Moose was strong—and stupid. Nothing could stop him as he carried the screaming Jessie through the gates of the stadium.

The other football players picked up on Jimbo and Crusher's lead. They searched the ground for bottles, cans, rocks and stones—anything they could use to fight and kill. They descended upon the creatures like locusts.

In this kind of mob scene, it didn't matter whose

side you were on. People lashed out at anyone in their path. Women and children were the easiest targets. They went down easily. And if any man looked the least bit monstrous, he was a target, too.

The mob flowed out of the bleachers and spread across the field like a plague. They went after the monsters and attacked them with whatever weapons they had—their cameras, their steel coffee containers, their Thunder Lake banners—whatever inflicted pain.

And as some of the monsters slipped out of the stadium, the mob began to storm the gates.

Fear turned into fury. Fury turned into rage. Rage became violence, and violence ruled the night. Every emotion that every person kept bottled up inside, day after day, came rushing out in one relentless storm. It was as if the Thunder Lake dam had burst—and the flood was their anger.

It was the anger people have for feeling helpless and afraid, lonely and depressed, shunned and ignored. It was the same rush of emotion that swept through the hearts and souls of Frankenstein's monsters.

Maybe that's why the mob wanted to kill them . . .

They saw themselves reflected in the monsters' eyes.

They surrounded Josh like a hungry swarm of insects, buzzing and biting, clawing his stitches, scratching his flesh. Josh screamed in pain and pushed his way through. But the people kept coming, more and more of them—an endless sea of hate and rage.

He saw Heather through the fence, holding Sara in her arms. She glanced at Josh, laughed and hissed, then carried her away into the darkness.

"*SA . . . RAAA!!!*"

The pain inflicted by bottles and cans and sticks and stones was no match for the pain in Josh's heart. He howled with anguish, knowing he had lost the battle . . .

The battle between life and death.

And it was about to get worse.

An ordinary housewife named Fran McDowell led the mob through the next stage of the riot. She was an uncommonly sweet woman who liked to read Tarot cards. She lived with her daughter on Longview Drive and knitted her own sweaters.

She was normally opposed to violence. She even wrote a letter once to a TV station to complain about one of their cop shows. But tonight, for some reason, she got swept up in the madness—and fought like a dog.

In fact, Baskerville was the first monster she went after. She grabbed the black hound by the tail and pulled with all her might. Baskerville yelped—and ran away. But Fran McDowell had only just begun to fight.

Her greatest victory was a one-on-one with Josh's father, a tall skinny zombie who looked like he'd break in two if you hit him hard enough. Fran joined a crowd of people who circled around him, taking turns punching and kicking. Fran watched for a minute, then pushed a few people aside—and went after the rotten stinking zombie herself.

She meant to pull his hand behind his back and hold him in an arm lock . . .

But she never expected his gray bony arm to snap off in her hands.

The crowd roared and cheered. Fran held the arm high over her head and danced around the bonfire. Then, shrieking like an Indian warrior, she tossed the arm into the flames.

"Look!" she cried triumphantly. "They burn! They burn! These monster devils burn!!!"

The crowd swarmed around the giant bonfire, reaching in and grabbing sticks and boards and other pieces of wood. The makeshift torches were brandished with feverish delight and passed around from hand to hand. Within minutes, every man, woman, and child held a burning torch in their hands. The stadium glowed with a thousand points of light . . .

Fire.

The monsters fled in terror, ripping through the chain link fence as if it were made of paper.

And the mob followed them into the darkness.

They couldn't let these creatures get away. They knew what they had to do.

The thought was in everyone's mind. The word was on everyone's lips. And soon, the rhythmic chant rose up from the stadium and flowed through the gates— a thousand voices joined together, ringing out in the night as the torches waved and the angry mob took to the streets . . .

"Kill! Kill! *Kill! Kill! KILL! KILL! KILL!*"

21

Inferno

From the diary of Sara Watkins . . .

I'll never forget that night as long as I live.

It felt like the end of the world. The final battle between life and death, good and evil, right and wrong.

But perhaps that's too simple of an explanation. Is anyone totally good or totally evil? Isn't every monster worthy of human love . . . and every human capable of monstrous hate?

These questions will haunt me for the rest of my life. There are no easy answers that come to mind . . .

Only memories of thunder and lightning.

And the final, merciless scourge of fire.

Maybe someday, I'll forget that night in November, when all my hopes and dreams were burned to the ground.

Maybe someday, my tears will douse the flames.

Sara Watkins floated in a black void.

It was a vast, empty place, a no-man's-land between life and death, dreams and nightmares, hope and fear. She felt herself drifting in this realm of the unconscious, wondering how to escape—and not even sure if she wanted to. It was peaceful here. No death. No love. No pain.

But then she remembered the boy with green eyes. *Josh* . . .

And she knew she had to come back to the real world.

Slowly she opened her eyes . . .

And stared up at the ceiling of the old mill.

It took a moment to realize she was strapped down on the lab table. She couldn't move her arms and legs. The leather straps cut into her wrists and ankles. But she could move her head—so she turned and looked at the grisly scene around her . . .

Jessie and Eddie struggled in the arms of the Morgan brothers, who held them so tightly that the teenagers' faces turned red. Moose Morgan blubbered and drooled on Eddie's shoulder. Mike brushed his cracked yellow lips back and forth across Jessie's neck. The dead duo grunted and cooed like giant, grotesque infants, fondling their favorite toys.

Heather Leigh Clark sat in front of the computer equipment, staring at her reflection in the screen. She raked her nails through her yellow-green hair—and smeared red blood over her mouth like lipstick.

The floor was littered with wriggling body parts— the broken remains of Grandfather Frank's final, failed creation. The devil-dog scampered from one piece to another, lowering its hideous human head and sniffing a white hairy hand, a brown arm, a leg . . . then it looked up and saw Sara staring at it.

The monster-dog-thing bared its teeth—and dashed

across the room toward her. It jumped up and placed its black front paws on the lab table. Then it lowered its gray human face inches away from Sara's—and licked her.

Sara screamed . . .

And Grandfather Frank laughed.

"Down, boy, down!" he snapped at the hybrid creature, pushing it off the lab table, then sneering. "This one belongs to me."

Sara looked up at Grandfather Frank—and gasped. His face was streaked with dried blood, his eyes gleaming with madness. His neck was torn open, the steel splints barely holding his head up. And his gnarled hand waved a scalpel in front of her face.

Sara tried to think fast. "If you kill me," she whispered, "who will perform surgery for you? You need me, Grandfather Frank . . . for my hands."

The old man tilted back his gruesome head and laughed. "You think you're so special, Sara?" he cackled. "There will always be others. There will always be bright, young scientists willing to explore the unknown. You can never stop progress."

"You call this *progress*?" Sara gasped. "That mess on the floor is *progress*? That dog with a two-hundred-year-old human head is *progress*?"

Grandfather Frank pressed the scalpel to Sara's lips. "Quiet!" He scowled. "Your moral conscience bores me. There is no such thing as right and wrong, Sara. There is only truth. Cold, scientific truth. When I resurrect you, I'll have to cut that silly schoolgirl passion out of your brain. All your talk of love everlasting. See if it saves you from the final truth of *death*!"

He grabbed an IV stand with a hanging bottle of blue artificial blood, then hooked up a tube and needle.

"*This* is the only thing that will save you, Sara. Not *love*." He spit the word out and reached for another tube. "But first, I have to drain your blood."

Sara winced as he inserted a huge needle in the tube and touched the point to her throat. She closed her eyes, gritted her teeth . . .

And the door to the mill burst open.

The ravaged corpses of Josh and Jessie's parents stumbled into the lab, their eyes blazing with terror. The father had lost his arm, and the mother clung to his side, weeping. They'd been badly beaten. The gray flesh was torn from their bones.

Grandfather Frank dropped the needle to the floor and limped across the room. Then he looked out the door—and saw the twinkling lights of a thousand torches swarming along the edge of the lake. The voices of the mob rose up in the night . . .

They were out for blood.

"The fools!" snapped Grandfather Frank. "They think they can halt the progress of science! Impossible! I've seen their kind before . . . angry, stupid people who destroy things they can't understand."

He turned and glared at Jessie and Eddie, then Sara on the lab table. The sounds of the mob grew louder, their torches blazing. Soon, they would storm the mill.

"There's no time to lose," the old scientist muttered under his breath. "I'll have to do this quickly."

He grabbed a scalpel from the table and turned

to Sara. Then raising the sharp instrument high in the air, he staggered forward, ready to plunge it into her chest.

Sara closed her eyes and screamed.

She waited for the sickening jolt of steel against flesh, plunging, piercing, penetrating her heart. But it never happened . . .

Because Josh burst into the mill.

And tackled Grandfather Frank to the floor.

"Josh!!!"

Sara cried out with all the passion and terror in her soul. Then she burst into tears—and watched as the mill exploded with violence . . .

The monster-dog jumped on top of Josh, sinking its yellow teeth in his neck. Josh howled with pain and threw the beast across the room, where it knocked Eddie and Moose Morgan to the floor. In a flash, Eddie was up and fighting, pulling Jessie free from the clutches of the monstrous Mike. The Morgan brothers roared and staggered after the two teenagers, who ran to the corner of the room.

Sara watched in horror as Josh's zombie parents ganged up on their resurrected son. The mother and father knocked Josh to the floor and pinned him down. Then Heather Leigh Clark pounced on his head, dragging her nails back and forth over his face.

Jessie screamed in the corner. Sara looked over to see Eddie trying to protect Jessie from the Morgan boys, swinging a heavy chain over his head. For a split second, he glanced at Sara. She could see the desperation in Eddie's eyes—and his love and concern.

"Run!" Sara screamed. "Get out of here! Don't worry about me, just *run!*"

Eddie and Jessie moved slowly toward the open door of the mill. The Morgan boys bobbed and ducked as Eddie lashed out with the chain. Soon they were right in front of the door. But Eddie wasn't ready to leave without Sara. He couldn't abandon her, not now, not ever.

But then something happened that forced Eddie and Jessie out the door . . .

The monster-dog attacked.

Snarling and snapping, the unholy beast charged and jumped—knocking Eddie and Jessie through the doorway and into the night. They rolled across the ground outside the mill, kicking and fighting for their lives. The creature was relentless. It snapped at their fingers and clawed at their bodies. Jessie screamed when she saw its jaws clamp down on Eddie's throat . . .

And she cheered when Baskerville saved him.

The big black hound came charging out of the darkness, leaping on top of the hell-beast and knocking it to the ground. Jessie scrambled to her feet and helped Eddie up, then stood back and watched the battle of the monster dogs.

Baskerville sank his fangs into the stitches of the beast-thing's neck. The creature roared in pain and tried to pull away. But Baskerville wouldn't let go. The family dog seemed determined to rip that gray ugly head right off the monster's canine body.

Then a bloodcurdling sound rose up in the night— an eerie chorus of voices that made Jessie and Eddie turn and look across the shore of Thunder Lake . . .

"Kill! Kill! *Kill! Kill!*"

A thousand torches waved in the air like a swarm of angry fireflies. A giant, shapeless, living thing, the mob ebbed and flowed across the shoreline, gaining strength and momentum as it swept along the edge of the lake—and descended on the mill.

Suddenly there were people everywhere, screaming and hollering. Somebody pointed at Baskerville and the dog-creature, yelling out, "There they are! The monsters! Get 'em!!!"

The beast with the human head broke away from Baskerville and dashed into the mill. But Baskerville ran in after him.

"Baskerville, NO!!"

Jessie screamed, but it was too late. Her dog disappeared into the mill, and mobs of people knocked her aside, waving their torches and shouting. Jessie stumbled backward and grabbed onto Eddie. Then she watched in helpless horror as the frantic crowd surrounded the mill.

A single voice rose up from the mob, a voice that made Jessie's blood run cold . . .

"Burn them!! Burn the monsters!! Burn them to the ground!! *Burn them all!!*"

Then the single voice became a thousand voices, united as one . . .

"Burn! Burn! *Burn! Burn! BURN! BURN! BURN!*"

Jessie cried out in horror, the tears in her eyes blurring the orange glow of torches into one ball of flame. Eddie reeled from shock—and exploded, breaking away from Jessie and pushing his way through the crowd.

"No!!" he screamed. "Don't do it! Stop!" He cried as he struggled to make himself heard, his tears fueling his rage. *"Don't burn it! Sara's still in there! NOOOO!!!"*

But it was too late.

Someone threw the first torch onto the roof of the mill, and one after another, a thousand blazing torches were cast upon the old wooden structure.

The dried, cracked walls were the first thing to burn, the flames lapping the side of the building and curling upward. Then the fire spread across the roof, creeping higher and higher until it engulfed the small tower on top. Soon, the whole place was a blazing inferno. Even the waterwheel burned, the slow-turning paddles flickering orange and yellow as the water splashed across the burning wood.

It all happened so fast, Eddie hardly had a chance to breathe. The mill was on fire. And Sara was trapped inside. Sara . . . the girl he loved . . . the girl he'd die for . . .

Eddie tilted back his head and roared in anguish and shock and pain . . .

"Saraaaa!! NOOOOO!!!"

And screaming at the top of his lungs, he pushed his way through the mob. And entered the burning mill.

Sara lifted her head off the lab table and coughed, choking on the thick black smoke that filled the room. She could hardly see anything—just glimpses of monsters rising and falling in the billowing blackness.

This is what hell looks like, she thought. And this is where I'm going to die.

Suddenly she saw Josh's mother and father streak across the room in flames. They screamed as they burned, then disappeared into the smoke. Then she saw Heather Leigh Clark with her hair on fire. She screeched, hissed—and melted to the floor like the Wicked Witch of the West.

Sara cried out in vain, the smoke burning her eyes, the heat scalding her flesh.

Baskerville howled in the blackness. With a loud snap of his jaws, something fell to the floor and rolled toward the lab table. Sara looked down . . .

It was the dismembered head of the original Frankenstein monster.

Before Sara had a chance to scream, a terrifying sound rose up from the smoke. It was the most savage roar she'd ever heard, and she knew it was Josh. She turned her head and caught a fleeting glimpse of her resurrected boyfriend . . .

He was tearing the Morgan brothers limb from limb.

Sara closed her eyes to block out the horrible sight of arms and legs flying through the air. She surrendered her mind to darkness, and tried not to think about how she was going to die. She thought about Eddie—and how much she really loved him.

If she thought hard enough, she could even see his face and hear his voice . . .

"Sara."

The voice wasn't in her head. It was real. Sara opened her eyes to see Eddie standing over her, his face blackened with soot.

"Eddie! What . . . ?"

"Shhh." He grabbed a scalpel and sliced the leather straps that bound her wrists and ankles. Then he pulled her up, into his arms.

"Eddie . . ." Sara sobbed as she leaned against him. Then, together, they stumbled through the black smoke toward the door of the mill. Tears burned her eyes as she clung to the boy she'd grown to love. And terror gripped her soul when she saw the man she'd grown to hate . . .

Grandfather Frank was blocking the doorway.

"Die with me." He leered, grinning madly. "Die with me, my children."

Sara screamed. But Eddie didn't even blink—he simply reached up and tore away the steel splint that supported Grandfather Frank's head, then shoved the old man aside.

As Eddie pulled Sara through the door, she couldn't help but turn and look—one last time—at the man who spawned a legend. Victor Frankenstein, himself. Now he was Grandfather Frank, and his head dangled and flopped from his neck like a dead fish. He tripped and fell on the floor—where he was attacked by the severed parts of his own monsters.

A hand with sharp fingernails dug into his chest. A leg wrapped around his neck. And the head of the original monster opened its jaws—and bit down on his nose.

Grandfather Frank screamed.

Then Sara was yanked away, pulled through the door by Eddie and thrust into the night, where the cold fresh air made her gasp and cough and sob . . .

"Eddie." She burst into tears and threw her arms around him. He stroked her hair and led her away from the building, away from the flames and the heat—and the foul smell of death. Then they turned and looked back at the mill. Something small and black ran out of the flames like a bat out of hell. It dashed through the crowd—and jumped on top of a short dark-haired girl . . .

"Baskerville!"

Jessie squealed with delight and hugged her dog, who showered her with kisses.

"Look!" Sara pointed. "It's Jessie and Baskerville! Come on!" She pulled Eddie through the crowd, rushing up and embracing her dearest, closest friend.

"You're alive, Sara!" Jessie gasped. "Thank God, you're alive! How did you get out of there?"

Sara threw her arm over Eddie's shoulder and kissed him on the cheek. "My hero," she said. Eddie blushed.

The three teenagers smiled through their tears as the crowd moved past them, spellbound by the sight of the burning mill. Then, slowly, the smiles faded from their faces. An overwhelming sadness swept over their souls.

In silence, they stared at the flames . . .

And thought about Josh.

They knew he was still in there, trapped in the inferno. He couldn't possibly survive the raging flames. But they knew that even after death, his love would live forever.

Josh . . .

Sara felt the pain in her heart. And she knew it

would never go away. For the second time in her life, she mourned Josh's death—mourned the boy who taught her how to open her heart and share her soul. But this time, Sara felt as if something else had died inside of her. Something she could never bring back to life.

The tears flowed down her face. She looked at Jessie and saw the pain in her eyes. Sara reached for her hand and held it. Neither one said a word. They didn't have to. They were sisters now. Blood sisters, bound by love and death and sorrow.

Then she turned to Eddie. Looking into his eyes, Sara knew he understood everything she'd gone through. He knew how much she loved Josh. And he knew she would never be able to forget him.

Sara took Eddie into her arms. She hugged him as hard as she could. She kissed him on the neck, on the cheek. Then she looked into his beautiful dark eyes— the eyes of a true friend—and whispered . . .

"I love you, Eddie."

He looked at her, unable to speak. But words weren't necessary. His kiss said it all. Their lips met, soft and warm, a simple expression of a deeper passion that touched their hearts and lifted their souls.

Then the three teenagers stared into the flames on the edge of the lake . . .

And said a silent prayer for Joshua Frank.

The creature stood in the doorway of the burning mill.

No one could see him there, amidst the fire and

smoke. He felt invisible. And that made the creature feel better. No one could see how ugly he was. Ugly, and different.

And alone.

The others were gone now. The dead ones. He was the only one left. The only one dead and alive at the same time.

He stood in the doorway and looked out at the crowds of people. He saw his sister and his dog. They looked happy. That was good.

Then he saw the girl with yellow hair, the girl he loved . . .

Sara.

She was standing with the boy. She was touching him, holding him, hugging him.

Then she kissed him.

Even through the smoke and flames, the creature could see the love between Sara and the boy.

Love.

The creature remembered love. Sara loved him when he was alive. Even now, she loved him. He could see it in her eyes and feel it in his heart. But death had changed him somehow. Death had taken over his brain. He could feel the dark clouds coming, the thunder and lightning. He knew he would never really be alive. Not anymore.

Sara belonged with the boy who kissed her.

And the creature belonged dead.

The smoke swirled in his eyes, and tears streaked his gray monstrous face. He looked out at a world filled with people, a world filled with love, and he knew he could never be a part of it.

He was a monster.

And death was his only hope.

Taking a step backward into the blazing light of the flames, he closed his eyes and sobbed.

He tried to remember things about his life. The sister he grew up with. The music he played. The girl he loved. He tried hard to remember it all—this thing called life . . .

But he couldn't do it.

Everything was lost now, like a dream. Gone forever.

The creature raised his hand and touched his face. He felt the stitches and scars, the neck bolts, the sunken bones beneath the skin. What was he? What was this *thing* he had become?

The thing that used to be Josh.

The flames rose up around him. So bright. So beautiful. Fire everywhere. Fire in his head. Fire in his soul. He reached into his pocket and touched the tiny gold ring. His heart pounded in his chest as he opened his mouth to speak—his last words.

"Love . . . you . . . Sa . . . ra."

Then, with tears in his eyes, the creature turned . . .

And walked into the light.

Epilogue

From the diary of Sara Watkins . . .

The nightmare is over.

The fire at the mill burned until dawn. I watched it from my bedroom window, unable to sleep until the last flame flickered and died. For the longest time, I thought it would burn forever . . . like my love for Josh.

Today was Thanksgiving. Eddie and his parents joined me and Jessie for our big family dinner. No one said a word about monsters or Homecoming or anything. No one dared. I think they saw the haunted look in our eyes—and the unspoken pain we shared. We told our parents and the police the names of everyone who died in the mill that night. The rest of the story we kept to ourselves. I wonder if I'll ever tell them.

Before dinner, my mom and dad asked Jessie if she'd like to come live with us. They wanted to become her legal guardians. I was thrilled to hear Jessie say yes. Now we'll be sisters by blood and by law.

Then we gathered at the table to offer our Thanksgiving blessings. As my dad was saying grace, I looked over at Eddie and Jessie—and I knew I had plenty to be thankful for. No one said a word when I started to cry.

After dinner, I took the flowers from the centerpiece and excused myself from the table. I said I wanted to take a walk by myself. I needed to be alone for a while. Then I left the house and walked along the edge of the lake. I didn't stop until I reached the blackened remains of the old mill. With tears in my eyes, I stepped over the ashes, thinking about love and death. And Josh. Then I placed the flowers on the charred earth and sang a few lines from one of Josh's songs . . . "the heart that beats forever, the love that never dies."

Now I understand the meaning of those words. Through me, Josh's love will grow with every person I share it with. And through them, his love will bloom for all eternity . . .

Like flowers in the ashes.

Thank you, Josh.

May you rest in peace.